THE

OBSESSION

An erotic tale of
Princess Shanyin

LILIANA LEE

PROLOGUE

History will not remember me kindly, nor do I want it to. The book of our dynasty will say many things about me: that I was cruel, that I was decadent and depraved. They will claim that my pleasures were perverse in nature. Let me tell you that these things are all true... and not true...

It is hard for me to say exactly what I found so arousing about Yuan. From the very first moment I saw him, I wanted him in every way, more than any lover before or since. He was standing in a sea of bureaucrats and retainers assembled before the Emperor, though it was he alone who caught my eye.

Yuan was buried among the midlevel officials, yet he stood so tall and proud that it was impossible not to notice. He was young for such a position as well, perhaps only a few years older than myself. Fire shot through my veins at my first glimpse of him. As he watched the proceedings in the imperial hall, I detected a hint of defiance in the set of his jaw. His eyes were black and hard and my sex flooded when he glanced in my direction.

I leaned forward in my seat to address the Emperor on his throne. "Who is that?"

Several pairs of eyes fixed onto me from down below. I was one of the few in the empire allowed to address his Imperial Majesty so directly. The ministers of the court feared and hated me for that alone, imagining how I must whisper political schemes into his ear. But the Emperor was my younger brother and the things we said to each other were usually for our own amusement.

This time, Ziye actually looked impatient at my interruption. He took the throne when he was only sixteen years old after our father passed away. He was seventeen now.

"Who?" he asked me.

I gave a quick gesture with my hand. My brother knew immediately who I was interested in. And why.

"Lord Chu Yuan," he answered with a smirk. "You're shameless, Elder Sister."

Our conversation held up the entire court. Ziye turned his attention back to the elder official standing at the foot of the dais and I did as well. I had little interest in affairs of government, but when Ziye summoned me, I could hardly refuse.

The gray-haired bureaucrat was reading from a long sheet of paper.

"Continue," Ziye commanded.

As the official read, his voice began to tremble. I tried to recall the details of the situation. My brother had called this man to the front to read from a letter one of the imperial eunuchs had intercepted. I listened with a touch more interest—oh, the letter mentioned Ziye and it was not very flattering. The assembly grew deathly quiet.

My attention wandered once more to the handsome Yuan. For a moment, his gaze rose to the throne and my heartbeat ran wild. Such fire in that look! I couldn't wait to get him alone.

"So you question my ability to rule," my brother was saying.

His voice rang to the very back of the audience hall. Tension rippled throughout the assembly when he stood. "Does anyone else agree?"

Of course no one did. Most lowered their heads in supplication, afraid to meet the glittering eyes of this boy who was barely a man. Ziye had only been on the throne for a year, but his courtiers had learned quickly. Even I held my breath as he descended the dais.

The official prostrated himself, pressing his forehead to the hard floor. He rambled an apology: this humble servant was mistaken, he was sorry, he was worthless.

"Tell me Minister He, who do you think should be on this throne instead?"

The official was given no chance to reply. Ziye's foot shot out and the sickening crack against Minister He's skull could be heard throughout the hall. My stomach lurched, but I froze. The entire assembly remained deathly still while Ziye kicked the old man again and again, as if the minister were no more than a dog.

"Who was this letter intended for?" he demanded.

My brother's personal bodyguards gathered at the edge of the dais, but not to stop the brutal beating. They were ready should anyone try to interfere. I winced as Ziye's foot snapped into the minister's ribs.

"Imperial Majesty!"

Mine was the only voice in the hall and Ziye stopped immediately. I rose to my feet to descend the steps, but my knees were water. My chest constricted so tight I co hardly breathe.

Ziye's face was so contorted with rage, I could barely recognize it. Yet his eyes glowed. His face was alight.

I glanced downward as I took his side. "Look, there's blood on the Emperor's shoe," I complained.

Ziye followed my gaze. "Right," he said after a pause. "We must keep up appearances."

The offending minister was dragged away and the court adjourned immediately after. As the ranks filed, I sought another glimpse of Lord Chu Yuan. His jaw was clenched. His eyes were shuttered and unreadable and the tight fist in my chest slowly unfurled. The sick feeling in my belly faded to be replaced with a low, throbbing ache.

Outside in the courtyard, I sent one of my eunuchs to him while my pulse raced. Usually I would just issue an official summons and wait in my personal palace, but today I watched as my messenger approached.

Yuan shook his head with a harsh curl of his lip. The look of disdain on his face made my blood run so hot that it boiled in my veins. I swore by my very last breath that I would have him; I would have that strong body beneath me, undone and throbbing inside me. In every way under heaven.

They tell stories of how insatiable I was in the bedchamber. My bed itself was legendary. Carved from rosewood, it was said to be spacious enough to accommodate my entire harem. That fable wasn't true, but I did have ten join me once, surrounding me as if I were the center of a lotus flower. Closing my eyes, I lost track of hands and mouths and tongues as they worshiped my body.

So many at one time was entirely too cumbersome. I found that two suited me quite well. Perhaps three at times. Which one, or two, or three I chose each night depended on my mood.

Each of their names was listed on a tile. Every evening, I turned over the ones I wanted to summon to my chamber the same way the Emperor did in his harem.

Tonight, I didn't look at the names as I made my selections. There were times I preferred they remain nameless so I wouldn't be distracted from my pleasure, but there was a particular reason I didn't want any names or even faces this evening. Yuan occupied my every thought and desire.

My maidservants undressed me and let my hair down before departing. I lay on the magnificent bed face down with my head resting on my hands. A sheer curtain hung around the frame, dimming the glow of the lanterns.

Then I closed my eyes and waited.

My lovers would come to me, sometimes one at a time, sometimes all at once. They would never keep me waiting too long. Just long enough to make my skin tingle with anticipation.

I sensed a presence in the chamber before I felt the touch on my body. The first contact was upon my back. It was a gentle, soothing stroke that traveled down my spine, then up again to round my shoulders. Strong hands. I sighed and arched into them. My muscles had begun to grow lax and my flesh warm when another hand circled my ankle. A thumb ran down my instep, making me flinch. *Insolence.* I hated being teased in such a way. I was about to turn around when the perpetrator pressed his lips to my heel in supplication before stroking his hands up my calves.

He was being bold, this one. I accepted it for now. He was doing it to make my pulse rise and to heighten the moment. A few of my concubines occasionally showed some initiative. I had to admit, sometimes willfulness had its advantages.

The myriad of hands were stroking me in broad circles, over my neck, my shoulders, my back. Slowly they worked my legs apart to massage my inner thighs. My breathing slowed and grew deeper. I could hear the men breathing heavy all around me as they readied me.

There was one more. He hadn't yet made his presence known and I wondered when he would join us. I didn't have to wonder for long. There was a shifting of weight on the bed and then a hand moved between my legs. Gentle fingers parted my sex and then the touch—oh, that first perfect touch. Not too soft and not too rough.

I imagined Yuan's long fingers there, caressing me for

the first time, and a flood of wetness poured from me. The fingers slipped through to explore deeper while the other hands continued to knead over my limbs. My body was being soothed as well as primed for sex at the same time.

One finger entered into me, curving upward as it penetrated. Yuan again. He would know how to pleasure a woman, wouldn't he? In my mind, I saw his face and imagined the hard set of his jaw as he glared at me in disapproval, which only made me hotter.

I would have him and it would be all the sweeter because of his initial resistance. I imagined him pleasuring me now with that look of disdain and condemnation. He didn't want to do it, but he had no choice.

I moaned. The sound was muffled by my arm, but my lovers had heard me. The hands turned me over and my heart pounded. The mouth that covered my breast was also Yuan's. As was the one kissing a line down my stomach. Another mouth was at my neck, nibbling then biting. They were becoming more insistent. They were slaves summoned for my pleasure, but they were still men and subject to their own needs as well.

When I was feeling wicked, I would hold them off and take my own pleasure while tormenting them. But I had been in a fever since Yuan had refused me. I lifted my hips to urge my lovers on.

A tongue flicked over my nipple and my body pulled tight, all sensation concentrating on that single point. I pressed myself to the source of the pleasure, demanding more. Whoever he was, he gave me what I wanted while his hand squeezed my other breast. I reached out to seek another concubine and dragged him down, kissing him hungrily. I wanted the intimacy of mouth against mouth tonight. I wanted everything.

Right then, someone wrapped his hands around my thighs and held them open. Instead of lowering himself to me, he lifted me up to him. My sense of balance was disrupted right before his mouth closed over me and his tongue penetrated my sex. *Yes.* He licked upward to search out the apex of my desire, the small knob of flesh that was throbbing for attention. He found it and circled with just the tip of his tongue, filling me with waves of pleasure.

Yuan was with me again; as haughty and beautiful as he'd been in the Emperor's court. I squeezed my eyes shut. In my mind, my male concubines were holding him by the arms, pressing Yuan's head down between my legs to force him to taste me. That image and the quick flutter of a tongue over my pearl was all I needed to reach my climax. It shot through me like lightning and I had to bite down to keep from calling out Yuan's name. The name of the one man I wanted, but had yet to conquer.

When I opened my eyes there was a shadow above me. I couldn't see his face, but I could hear the strain in his voice.

"Princess!" he pleaded.

Instead of speaking, I curved my legs around his hips and he sank into me, stretching out my already sensitive flesh. The penetration almost reached the point of pain before he retreated, moving back and then forward again in a shallow thrust. He found a rhythm and I lifted toward him in approval.

They all knew what I liked. The entire harem would be punished if I was disappointed. Sometimes I had them punished even after I'd fallen asleep sated. It was good for them to not become too complacent.

I felt him quicken above me, his muscles straining to hold back. I wouldn't come again so soon, but I still enjoyed the rush of passion that overtook a man in the moment right before release. There was a rawness, a desperation to it that I loved. I looked into his face, enjoying the strain, the look there that bordered on pain.

With a groan, the slave pulled out of me and spilled upon the pallet. I hadn't given him permission to lose his essence inside me.

Another moved to replace the first. His organ slid into me in a long stroke that made me gasp. He was larger. Thicker. I might have recognized this one by the feel of him alone. Rather than thrusting deep, he ground his hips in a circle that made wonderful things happen inside of me. I closed my eyes and let my head fall back decadently. He would bring me to another climax, I willed it so. We strained toward it together, my nails digging deep into his shoulders until I was overcome.

My body was exhausted when the last organ entered me. He tried to please me as best he could, but I was no longer interested. I pushed him away and he withdrew without protest. I dismissed all but one, the one with the talented mouth who had brought me to my first climax.

He licked me slowly, lovingly, as I fell to sleep. He was

able to bring me once more to a peak, but it was only a small release, a whimper rather than a scream. I should have been satisfied. My concubines had performed well that night, but I was unfulfilled.

I was still agitated, my mind churning from my confrontation with Yuan. He was what I wanted to remember from this day. Not the blood, not the violence in the imperial assembly. Instead, I thought of Yuan's strong body and his proud, handsome face while I plotted how to make him mine. This was the final thought I took with me as I drifted away. Even while I slept, I continued to dream in fits and starts, my mind refusing to let me rest.

CHAPTER ONE

People like to tell a story about me and my imperial brother, and how I came to possess a harem. I lamented to Ziye once, after he took the throne, about the hardships of being a woman.

"Though our genders are different, we have the same father," I pointed out. "Yet you have more than ten thousand woman in your palace for your pleasure, while I am only allowed one husband. That is hardly fair."

Amused by my audacity, the Emperor gifted me with thirty male concubines, my cherished and skilled harem of lovers.

Oh, what a wicked, immoral woman I am. And how perverse my brother was for indulging me.

Seven years separated my brother Ziye and me, though we were both born of the same mother; my father's Empress. Our lineage is an illustrious one. Our father became Emperor after killing his own brother who had previously taken the throne by assassinating their father.

My brother had always been a pawn because of that piece of flesh between his legs. Our father's enemies pondered over whether they should have him killed as easily as they pondered over what to have for dinner. He was a son, capable of ascending the throne, seeking revenge, waging war and beheading their sons. No one is more dangerous to royalty than our own families.

Ziye, after surviving so many plots, gained a rather twisted perspective on how fleeting life was as well as how he should make good and frequent use of his male organ while he was still able. After all, the treacherous thing had caused him to be a target all his life.

Am I being kind by trying to explain his obsessions? I am rarely kind, but I've witnessed how many times my brother was dangled before death. When he was a child of six and I thirteen, I held onto him in our dark prison cell while our uncle decided whether we should live or die.

I should tell you of another time, shortly after our father had claimed the throne, when I slipped into a senior official's bedchamber and removed my silk robe. I extinguished the lanterns and climbed onto his bed, allowing this stranger's hands to roam over my breasts and his thick organ to penetrate me. All so he would say a few choice words of praise for my brother in court.

So Ziye would then be named as crown prince. So we would be protected from our uncles and cousins and the other heirs who would destroy us.

Before you pity us, let me remind you that we survived. Now my brother is Emperor and I am Princess Shanyin. Once my brother ascended the throne, he remembered those indignities brought upon us. Like many emperors before him, he went on a killing spree, executing traitors and would-be traitors and powerful ministers who tried to tell him not to behead so many people.

Ziye also takes who he wants, whenever he wants. When he's bored, he strips his palace women naked so he can chase them about the imperial garden. If a pretty daughter of some functionary catches his eye, he'll summon her immediately to his bed and insist to her family they should consider it an honor that the Emperor had shown them favor.

Palace gossipers claim Ziye harbors an unnatural attraction to me, his very own sister by blood. They've observed how his eyes wander lewdly over my body as he brags to me of his sexual exploits.

If this were true, what better way to shield myself from his attentions than with thirty young, strong, virile lovers? I couldn't very well ask for thirty armed guards against the Emperor, could I?

My handsome concubines sleep in my chamber. They surround me whenever the Emperor makes an excuse to visit me in private. I make a show of thanking him for his generous gift of my infamous harem, which ensures that I will never have to sleep alone.

And each night as they pleasure me, I take back every sexual favor, every touch I ever bartered away.

I have no illusions about Ziye's perverse tastes or how power has made him corrupt and obscene. My brother is absolutely depraved.

But so am I.

"Thirty lovers aren't enough for you?" Ziye asked with a laugh when I made my request the day after seeing Yuan in court.

Though striking, Yuan was not the most beautiful man I'd ever seen, but since he'd refused my invitation I was unable to think of anyone else. I had to have him.

"It would amuse me, brother, if you sent him to my palace."

"Lord Chu Yuan is not some lowly retainer. He's of noble birth," Ziye replied.

"As are some of your favorite concubines," I countered. "Don't you tire of sleeping with slaves?"

My Emperor brother chuckled at that, and I knew he would indulge me.

"And I can give you my full report on his loyalty to the throne. Most men can't keep a secret in bed," I added sweetly.

Ziye regarded me unblinking. "I will grant him to you for ten days," he conceded finally. "Just so you can tire of him faster."

There was a raw edge of jealousy beneath his breath, but I didn't let it worry me. Ten days was more than enough to satisfy my curiosity for any man. Ziye was right, I would probably tire quickly of Yuan. For the moment, I was elated.

That evening, I couldn't swallow a single bite. I waved away dish after sumptuous dish as my stomach fluttered like a bird in a cage. Sleep wouldn't come, yet I passed by the row of harem tiles more than once, not turning a single one.

What had come over me? I was nervous, fearful, vibrating with anticipation of the moment Yuan would appear before me. The thought of it stole my breath. Every inch of my skin ached with yearning.

I wouldn't feed this hunger gnawing inside me. Not tonight. For once, I denied myself all the pleasures and comforts I'd come to expect as if they were air and water. I wanted to be empty and wanting when the object of my infatuation came to kneel before me.

Infatuation; that was it. I was besotted like a fresh-faced young scholar. A lovesick maiden.

Yuan was an infection inside me. I lay awake, thinking of the hard line of his jaw and the only slightly softer curve of his mouth. The breadth of his shoulders. His hands. Had I truly looked at his hands? Were they as well-formed and strong as I envisioned them now? All this from a single look and now I was filled with a raging hunger, rendered trembling and weak.

Just past the second hour, in the deep darkness of the night, I called for a bath. Maidservants attended me and I let myself sink into the steaming water anointed with oils of cinnamon leaf and rosewood. The heat of the bath was another scourge upon my skin, cleansing me for my awaited visitor, as if I could be rendered pure and empty to be filled.

Afterward, I reclined in my bedchamber, anointed with perfume oil. The sun had not yet risen, yet my body was awake. The womanly cleft between my legs was swollen and damp and I clenched my hands into fists to keep from touching myself.

The sweet pain of waiting! I reveled in it. It would make the union of our bodies so much more powerful.

I summoned Yuan to my Eastern Palace at the fifth hour. He didn't appear before me until well into the next double hour, sauntering into the audience hall with the same haughty air I remembered.

He stopped at the prescribed distance from the dais to bow. Every movement appeared outwardly correct, except he dared to meet my eyes briefly before his head lowered. A challenge. Defiance radiated out from him even as he remained on his knees.

We were alone. I had sent all my attendants away and my guards awaited outside the chamber, ready to storm in should I require them. But why should I? Yuan was merely a lowly subject and I was Princess Shanyin.

"Do you always answer an imperial summons with such lack of care?" I asked coolly.

His head remained bowed, hands to the ground. "This subject responds to all important matters with haste."

"Then my command carries no importance to you?"

I expected at least some mockery of an apology, but Yuan's lack of even a show of obedience angered me to no end. Heat rose up the back of my neck and I had to force my tone to remain light.

As light as the touch of a razor blade.

"I deemed the princess's request was not the most urgent task needing attention at the time."

"What does it matter if it was urgent?" I straightened on my seat. "There are over a thousand subjects within the imperial palace, each one the same as the next. An adequate number of servants to handle whatever else you deemed was more worthy of your attention."

"This subject humbly accepts whatever punishment the princess chooses for him."

His words weren't humble in the least. Yuan spoke as if he didn't take me seriously and that he was the one in command.

I was in an ill mood. The sheer insolence of his manner had cooled my desire. This wasn't how I had envisioned our meeting, bickering at each other with petty complaints.

Unknown to him, he had taken me in countless different ways since our first brief encounter. In my fantasies, he had brought me to my climax time and again until I wept for mercy. His thick organ had filled me like no other. I had imagined his face on all of my lovers while I bit down hard on my lip to keep from crying out Yuan's name. And yet here he was before me. Unaffected.

I was ashamed of the power he had over me when he had yet to lay a finger on me.

"Take off your clothes," I demanded, feeling the need to exert my authority.

With only a moment's hesitation he reached for the belt at his waist, tugging it free in two harsh movements. I reclined in my seat, head thrown back to watch with my arm draped lazily over one knee.

He didn't disobey, but there was defiance in the very

manner with which he complied. Tension rippled along his shoulders. His black eyes remained on me as he disrobed, layer by layer. He let the clothing fall away where he stood and my mouth went dry watching him, though outwardly I remained impassive.

His torso appeared before me, cut from stone and bronzed to perfection. I let my eyes roam over the hard contours of his shoulders, the width of his chest. He reached for the ties of his trousers, still watching me as I was watching him. Did I catch a hitch in his breath? The knot in his throat lifted and lowered as he pulled at the strings, the muscles of his arm flexing just so with the movement.

I stood. Yuan's jaw hardened as I approached and the cords on his neck pulled so tight they could snap. I could see how much it shamed him to undress before me. His fury was barely contained beneath the surface.

With that, my frustration dissipated and my blood heated again. Yuan was no longer unaffected. Fury and passion were close cousins.

He let the trousers fall, sliding past his hips to pool at his feet. His organ drooped heavily toward the ground, half-erect. I said nothing. He knew I could see it all, the evidence of his stirring desire. I raised my hand, stroking my fingers lazily beneath my chin as I openly contemplated him. It would be a lie to say I found him lacking.

Was his breathing growing deeper, against his most valiant efforts? Surely I'd only imagined it. Yuan couldn't be making this so easy.

I realized I had gone too long without issuing the next command. What would I do with all this masculine strength and beauty? I longed to take his sex in my mouth and feel it harden to its full potential, but what good would that serve? Me, a princess, servicing him as if I were a harem concubine?

"Come forward."

He did as I asked, his jaw set in that same defiant manner. How I wanted to see him beg and weep to please me.

"Now follow me."

I led him naked from the hall, not once glancing over my shoulder to check for his compliance. I was confident in my authority. Insolent with it.

Heavy footsteps behind me told me he obeyed my command without question. I paraded him through the corridor, past the grim-faced guards and female attendants who immediately fell into a bow at my approach. I could hear their hushed murmurs as we passed.

Normally I would have frowned upon such gossip, but today I delighted in it. I knew Yuan could hear their whispers as well. He could feel their curious gazes upon him and know that it was I who was subjecting him to such indignity.

I pushed open the double doors to my private apartments and wove through the chambers to my bed. My personal maidservants scrambled to their positions, bowing obsequiously. I had come in unannounced, with a virile and handsome man at my heels.

The girls were young and untried, but they were far from innocent. They were *my* maidservants after all and the sight of a man at my heels was hardly strange. They stood to await my command, but I had none for them. Accordingly, they flitted away to the various nooks and corners as fast as they had appeared.

Inside the bedchamber, I strode directly to my notorious bed. It was nearly the size of a small pavilion and I arranged myself in a relaxed pose at the center of it, making the expanse of the bed appear obscene. Yuan stood at the edge, staring at me with his fists clenched at his sides. There was a flush beneath his skin that I attributed to anger rather than desire. His cock lay limp, supporting my conjecture.

"How will you be able to perform your duties in such a state?" I teased, with a glance slanted downward at his manhood.

Yuan didn't flinch. He really was a proud, proud man.

"With her vast experience, I assume the princess must have the means to remedy the situation." His jaw ticked. "Whether the subject is willing or not."

"I assure you, no man has been unwilling in this bed."

"Perhaps not in body."

I smiled then. "I know your kind. Righteous. Upstanding. *Moral*." The last word slid acidly off my tongue. "So full of control and self-denial. Yet in the dark, when no one is looking—those men fuck like demons."

He swallowed, but his expression remained rigid. Too rigid.

"So you're here against your will," I prompted, bored.

"I will do whatever is asked of me, Princess."

"Upstanding *and* self-sacrificing. Here to be corrupted by imperial decree."

"It is indeed only the Emperor's command that brings me here," he said through his teeth.

I rose up on my elbows, regarding him with interest. "Are you married, Yuan?"

A muscle ticked along his jaw. "I am not."

"Then are you harboring some great love in your heart? A young and innocent beauty you're devoted to?"

For just a moment, there was a break in his impenetrable surface. There and gone.

"No," he said finally.

"I know that you are only here on the Emperor's insistence, yet you're a man. I don't truly believe you find this duty—as you call it—very distasteful. But go on denying it. Deny it while you spill your seed upon this bed. It will only amuse me more."

"As I said, my body can be made willing—"

"But not your mind," I finished for him with a sneer. "I won't force myself onto you, Yuan. What a chore that would be!"

He frowned at me, his fists unclenching. "Then I can go?"

I laughed outright. "No, you cannot leave. You are at my service for ten days. That is more than enough time to persuade your mind as well as your body—if they are truly as separate as you claim."

"I will never give in to you," he declared.

It was perfect. A challenge. Though I had my willing and devoted harem, it was still a special thrill to seduce a man to his knees. To see him surrender to his baser urges.

"Come here," I commanded softly.

He ducked beneath the canopy, going onto his hands and knees to approach me. I could see the sleek contours of his muscles as he moved, at once graceful and fierce. A sense of power swelled within me to have Yuan naked and crawling toward me while I was fully clothed. He hated every moment. I loved it.

"Undress me." I laid my head back as he came up beside me. When I looked up, I felt suddenly vulnerable as he leaned over me. Such was the precarious balance of sex; whenever a lover pushed himself inside me, whenever I took pleasure from another's body, it was both power and subjugation at once.

As Yuan reached for my robe, the lightness of his touch surprised me. The contrast of our positions had confused him as well. For all his proud anger, for as much as I repulsed him, he was the sort of man who looked at a woman and couldn't help but see softness. I knew that merely by how he untied my sash; carefully, with none of the brusque anger with which he had undressed himself.

To avoid looking at my face, Yuan stared instead at my body as he parted my robe. He didn't even undress me fully, instead only pulling the silk aside to reveal the embroidered bodice beneath.

"Touch me," I urged, the words scratching against my

throat. My breath came shallowly and all my anticipation in the dark of the night returned to me, warming my skin and pulling my nipples tight beneath the undergarment.

Where would he touch me? The first moment of skin against skin carried meaning. A touch to my face or neck would signal tenderness. Certainly there would be none of that. A touch to the hand would seem too affectionate. The feet, sensual. Intimately erotic. My shoulders—my breasts?

Yuan hesitated. His fingers still grasped the edge of my robe and suddenly I feared his decision. I shouldn't have given him so much power.

After a moment's pause, his hands lowered to the skirt that covered my legs. With his head bent, he pushed the thin material upward. There would be no slow, sensual exploration. He chose to serve me in the most expedient way possible.

I could hardly argue with that. Relaxing my limbs, I let my head fall back to await his hand.

The touch never came. I glanced up at Yuan and saw he had spied something on the bed. Reaching to the side of my pillow, he lifted up the smooth, elongated object carved from jade.

Ah, the jade phallus I had brought to me during my long hours of frustration the night before. I had left it by my pillow unused, choosing instead to prolong the wait. The phallus was intricately carved, with a broad, smooth tip that tapered down with a slight curve.

He finished pushing up my skirt and lowered the jade between my thighs, his face a mask above me. So this was his game—he loathed to touch me with his hands at all. No matter. The jade phallus was one of my favorite toys and I would still emerge triumphant, regardless of what game he tried to play.

I locked my gaze onto his face, but Yuan refused to look at me. The first touch of the cool jade against my sex sent a shudder through me. My legs opened of their own accord, my hips tilting upward. I had been waiting for this for so long.

Yuan directed the smooth tip over me and I bit down to keep from moaning. The jade slid easily along my flesh which was slick and swollen. I had expected his ministrations to be rough and laced with spite, which would have satisfied me regardless. Instead, the phallus moved in a slow, circular pattern, gathering moisture, making my hips churn with restless need.

So Yuan knew how to touch a woman. He knew the gentle rhythm that would render me weak and trembling. Each time the jade tip glided against the small pearl of my sex, a ripple of pleasure shot through me. My limbs grew rigid as I lifted my hips even higher.

Through slitted eyes, I searched out his face once more. His head was still bent, his expression focused and determined. His brow glistened with sweat and I could see his breathing had quickened. I couldn't resist glancing down, but with his legs bent as they were, his male member was hidden from me. It didn't matter. Every other sign showed that he was caught up in his task.

"Inside me," I whispered.

Another telling moment. Yuan knew how to perform this crucial act as well. The tip of the phallus centered onto me before easing slowly into my silken passage. I had expected to have to guide his hand, to show him exactly what I needed to be brought to climax. Instead I closed my eyes and concentrated on the feel of the smooth, hard stalk penetrating my flesh.

Yuan shifted positions, leaning closer to drive the phallus deeper. I imagined it was his cock thrusting into me instead of unyielding jade. Stone would never be as satisfying as flesh and blood, but for now it would do. It would do wonderfully.

Then he twisted the phallus inside me as he pulled outward and I did moan. Another twist as he pushed back in and I was in heaven. The ridges on the phallus teased against my inner walls, pleasuring me in ways no real organ could.

My hands had been clenched into the silk of my robe, but I reached out now to clasp Yuan's wrist. I don't know why I did it. I just needed some part of him to hold on to, but I regretted it immediately.

He froze, ceasing all that glorious sensation when I was at the edge of climax. My eyes flew open and I saw that he was looking directly at me, jaw clenched. Fighting against himself. I wanted to beg for him to continue, but instead I let my hand fall away. I squeezed my eyes shut.

After a moment, the phallus thrust deep into me and it wasn't long before my body found its rhythm once more. With a sharp cry, I shattered with pleasure, my hips rolling to prolong the moment.

Satiated, I let my body fall back onto the bed with loose limbs. A soft sigh escaped my lips.

Yuan moved beside me. I could feel him brush against me as he stretched himself out. All at once, my pulse quickened. Had this lover's service aroused him? Would he lower himself over me now and replace the jade with his own flesh?

The phallus remained inside me, though Yuan's hands were no longer guiding it. I felt his hot breath against my cheek before he spoke into my ear, his voice low.

"Is that all it takes, Princess?" he taunted.

My eyes flew open to find him close. Close enough to kiss me, but that was clearly not his intention.

"I believe that was no more than three minutes. Three minutes to make you sweat and scream."

I sat up, which only made me more aware of the weight of the carved stone still embedded in my sex. My robe hung partly open around my shoulders.

"How dare you—"

Yuan rose from the bed. It didn't matter that his cock was half-erect. For a moment, his words had filled me with shame, but I forced it out with anger.

"You bastard," I seethed. "You worthless slave."

His black eyes glittered at me and his smug expression said it all. I could call him whatever I wanted. He was the bastard, the demon, the beast that had rendered me helpless with desire. No matter that it was only for the space of a breath. No matter that this was the natural way of yin and yang and he didn't get to claim such superiority. No matter that it was exactly what I had demanded of him.

I dragged the phallus from my body and threw it at him. It missed his head and thudded against the wall behind him.

"Get out! *Get out!*"

I didn't care who heard me. This was my palace. There were my attendants and Yuan was here as my puppet to command. *Mine.*

If he had deigned to affect a bow, I would have torn him apart with my own hands. Instead Yuan said nothing and left as he had come. It was no consolation to me that he once more had to parade himself past the attendants naked. The glow from my orgasm had faded, stolen away by that bastard. And Yuan had dared to insult me. To turn what was my privilege and my triumph against me.

I wanted to order my guards to haul him back so I could have him flogged, but if I saw Yuan again at that moment, I would have probably had him killed. Instead I summoned the most well-endowed of my male concubines and worked him to exhaustion, taking what I wanted without a trace of shame.

CHAPTER TWO

I woke up the next morning to the stroke of hands soothing over my skin like water. My desperate hunger of the night before, fueled by my anger and humiliation, had been temporarily sated and now I rested languidly in the center of the spacious bed.

The hands on me became more insistent. Not to the point of roughness, just firm to the touch as they massaged over my legs, my arms, my breasts. I sighed, closing my eyes as I luxuriated in the flush of warmth.

Why had I allowed a few crude remarks from some underling to upset me? Yuan was exactly that. A lowly servant who had been granted temporary favor—favor that he chose to spit upon.

Strong arms lifted me from the bed and I smiled as I was laid back, my shoulders resting against a firm and muscular chest. It was my same lover from last night. Tai Jin was what I called him, or usually just Tai. The supreme. The most highly valued for how well-endowed he was and how well he pleased me.

I could feel the rise and fall of his breathing against my back as Tai took me by the hips. I did nothing more than lie there like a doll as he positioned himself beneath me. A moment later, I felt the thick head of his organ pushing into me from below.

With a sigh, I tilted my hips to urge him to enter me fully. He did so, stretching me once more until the sense of fullness brought me fully awake. By then, we had been joined by another from the harem. I didn't need to open my eyes to know who it was. Jiyi. Skill. I had bestowed that name upon him and skilled he was. His tongue swirled endlessly over my pearl while Tai's cock thrusted gently in and out of me.

The two of them often paired up and I suspected they were lovers. The days and nights were long while sequestered in the harem quarters and no other women were allowed there. There was an unspoken communication between them and they moved as if they were of one mind.

By the time Yuan was brought into the chamber, my two morning lovers had found the perfect rhythm, one thrusting into me from beneath while the other licked over me in long strokes.

The moment I sensed Yuan's presence beside the bed, my heart began to race. I slitted my eyes open to see him watching impassively, with his hands clasped behind his back. He was fully clothed in a dark robe without any adornment. His expression was a cool mask.

I said nothing to him. Instead, I stretched like a cat and concentrated on the soft, wet rasp of the tongue on my sex; the penetration of a hard cock inside me. And Yuan, forced to watch it all. I could see the pulse beating at his throat and the way his chest rose and fell. All the while, he granted me a hard, cold stare that was meant to rob me of any pleasure, but all it did was arouse me more. I let my head fall back against my lover's shoulder while keeping my gaze fixed on Yuan, letting my enjoyment show on my face. Tai's arms closed tighter around me as he deepened his penetration, rocking me toward heaven.

It was a long time before my climax took me over. I made sure to prolong it. To make Yuan stand there and witness every moment. My toes curled when the pleasure blinded me and I shuddered, sighing. Content.

Afterward, I took my time dismissing my darling concubines, and a maidservant brought a robe to drape over my shoulders. I cast a glance over at Yuan as I tied my sash. He was still standing beside the bed with his statue-like expression. How tiresome.

I breezed past him and felt a hint of satisfaction when he turned to follow obediently.

Out in the parlor, tea had already been set. The leaves steeped inside an ornate porcelain bowl. I beckoned for Yuan to sit across from me even though there was only one setting. His movements were stiff as he lowered himself onto the seat.

"Are you well in mind and body this morning, Yuan?"

"Was that display meant to tempt me?" he returned with disdain. "It had quite the opposite effect."

"Fool. I don't care about your pleasure or enjoyment. The only one I care to arouse is myself." I lifted the lid of the tea cup to take a sip, but not before I delivered an important message. "And I should inform you that if you ever make a petty attempt to insult me again as you did yesterday, I will simply have your tongue cut out."

I smiled, flushed with a heady mix of sex and power. Beneath the silk robe, sweat pooled on my skin and dripped between my breasts. The scent of my two lovers still lingered on me and I wondered if Yuan could smell them.

There was no reply, which I took as acceptance. What choice did he have, really? With that, I took my time sipping tea and nibbling lotus seed cakes while he watched me. With every moment that passed, Yuan became angrier and I more gleeful.

"You really do despise me," I remarked, darting the tip of my tongue over a fingertip to catch a crumb.

Again, no answer, but I could see the fierce glint in his eyes.

"I thought about having you whipped last night for your insolence. Hearing you beg for mercy would have put me in a better mood, but I realized the worst punishment I could bestow upon you was an entire day in my presence, with all my wickedness."

"Whatever you wish, Princess."

Stubborn, frustrating man. I shouldn't have promised not to force myself upon him. Then I could have him tied down and aroused before riding him until he shuddered and spilled his essence into me. That would take away that smug superiority of his. I could guarantee he would take less than the three minutes I had required.

I reached for my tea. The corner of my robe slipped from my shoulder as I drank and Yuan's gaze flickered to my bared skin before shifting away, as fast as the beat of a butterfly's wing.

His sense of modesty amused me greatly. As did his effort toward restraint.

"I want a bath," I declared, rolling my shoulders so the silk slipped further downward. "And you shall attend to me personally."

A haze of steam hovered over the bathing pool as I stepped into it. I sank down and reclined against the ledge until the water rose to my neck. Then I laid my head back against the edge of the pool, turning to meet Yuan's gaze expectantly.

He stood fully dressed in the damp, tepid air of the chamber, as if preparing for an audience in the imperial court. The steam had turned his dark blue robe to black. If he removed his shoes or official cap, he would be more comfortable, but he did none of those things. Instead he rolled up his sleeves, folding the material back in crisp movements.

I was fascinated by the muscled contours of his forearms as he reached for the washcloth.

"How did you get your appointment to the inner court?" I asked when he knelt beside the pool.

"I was promoted by Emperor Xiaowu for valor in service to the empire."

"Ah, a general in my late father's rebellion?"

"My father was the general. I merely followed his lead."

A soldier then, a former one. He looked to be perhaps four or five years older than I. Nearing thirty.

Yuan picked up a cake of pressed soapbean and concentrated on rubbing the soap into my shoulders and arms. His touch was rough, but I didn't mind.

"You fought against my uncle, then."

"Liu Shao was a usurper, without rightful claim to the throne," Yuan said.

Ziye had mistaken him for just another aristocrat. My brother hadn't known that Yuan's family had helped put us where we were now. It didn't change my plans in the least.

I was momentarily distracted as the washcloth ran down my arm, grazing the side of my breast. With an appreciative murmur, I closed my eyes and let myself sink deeper into the water. For the next few moments, all I could hear was the lap of the water against the side of the pools as Yuan washed my shoulders and arms. The cloth skimmed over my collarbone, deliberately avoiding my breasts.

But his hands were wonderfully strong and capable. His palms were slightly calloused, not the soft, pale hands of a courtier. It wasn't the first time I wondered how a pampered bureaucrat maintained such a physique, but now I knew he'd once been a soldier.

"It would be easier if you came into the bath," I suggested lazily.

Turning so I now faced the edge of the pool, I folded

my arms over the side and rested my head on them. The new position exposed my back and I waited for Yuan's ministrations to continue. After a moment's pause, a ripple in the water told me he had come into the bath as he was told. Opening one eye, I saw that Yuan was still fully clothed as he submerged himself.

With a snort, I closed my eyes once more. Let him be a fool. I had no care for his comfort.

Soon Yuan was beside me in the water, reaching for my shoulders. As his hands began to work at the knot of muscles in my neck, a shiver of unadulterated pleasure ran down my spine. The tension drained from my body and I went limp beneath his touch, luxuriating in the heat of the bath and the skilled workings of his hands.

I don't know why I ever considered that I needed to seduce Yuan to bed me in order to enjoy his services. I could have him attend to me like a slave, seeing to all my trivial needs. There was plenty of satisfaction that could be had.

"You know how to touch a woman," I murmured.

His hands hesitated upon my skin. I wondered if he'd remove his touch just to spite me.

"You're certainly no pale-faced youth," I went on. "Unsure of what to do with a woman's body."

There had been no hesitation yesterday when he'd pleasured me with the jade phallus. Even though he tried to shame me afterward, I knew how the act had made him hard.

Yuan continued my bath as if I'd said nothing. He ran

the cloth along my spine, following the curve of my back down, but then returning up again before dipping any lower. It could have been modesty, but it could have also been a tease. My breath came in shallow pants as I waited for him to run those miraculous hands all over me, over all the parts that were womanly and forbidden. In my palace, nothing was forbidden. At least not to me.

"Who was the first woman you took to bed?" I asked him.

I thought he would refuse to answer, but his reply came easy enough. "A courtesan."

That was typical for a young man of aristocratic blood.

"So she took *you* to bed," I teased, the corner of my mouth turning up wickedly.

"So she did."

Did I detect a hint of wistfulness? The washcloth traveled once more down my spine and followed the curve of my back to glide over my backside and thighs. I was kneeling in the bathing pool and I pulled my knees apart to give him access. Unfortunately, Yuan didn't take the invitation. He washed the back of my legs and then once more returned to my shoulders. By the end of the bath, my shoulders would gleam like polished ivory, they'd received so much attention.

"And then who else?" I pressed on. "Did you fall for your first lover or were there many others?"

"There were others. Courtesans...prostitutes."

He only hesitated for a moment before admitting the last part. Perhaps he had figured that the more easily he yielded to my smaller demands, the less I would antagonize him. He was being surprisingly accommodating—except for not allowing me to bed him.

I turned in the pool to face him. Yuan was soaked to the skin while still dressed in his robe. His official's cap had been removed and his hair hung long and damp against his face. There was a flush beneath his cheekbones that could just as easily be attributed to the heated water as it could be to other…things.

"Those women must have been very beautiful," I said.

"I hardly remember their faces."

Such restraint. The muscles of his jaw were pulled tight, his shoulders rigid just above the water. This conversation took more out of him than any sexual act I had demanded so far.

My eyes narrowed on him in challenge. "But there must be someone whose face you do remember."

Otherwise why would he be so determined to resist? Why not bed me like all of those other courtesans and prostitutes? I wouldn't even mind the comparison. Not when I considered him a plaything for my own desires.

He hesitated before replying. "There is no one."

I let his reply hang between us in the weighted air of the bath chamber. As I approached him, his breath hitched. Reaching for the front of his robe, I pulled him toward me, keeping my eyes locked onto his the entire time. Silently, I dared him to look away, but he wouldn't. He stared right back at me, his pupils black and hard.

His belt was also soaked through and difficult to work

loose in the water, but I managed without too much delay. I wasn't inexperienced either.

"You'll need new clothes," I said, pulling the robe open to expose his chest before releasing him. "Even I'm not cruel enough to have you walking around all day like a drowned rat."

For the rest of the morning, I had Yuan follow me about and stand by waiting while I performed the most mundane and inane of tasks. I strolled through my garden, which I visited every morning. It was summer and the flowers were in full bloom, filling the air with sweet perfume. I proceeded to inspect and touch every blossom while Yuan waited on me. My garden was my pride and joy; proof that even I could create something pure and beautiful.

Afterward, I had Yuan sit quietly and watch while I completed a brushwork painting I dedicated to the Emperor, may he live a thousand years. I visited the palace temple to light incense for every single one of my ancestors. Every single one, though I cared little for the lot of them.

Throughout these tasks, I barely spoke to Yuan. I was content to have him following at my heels, ensnared and unable to escape like he was my shadow.

So he despised me? Let him spend every waking moment of the day by my side.

When it was time for my midday meal, we returned to my chamber where I had course after course brought to me while I reclined upon the bed. Yuan sat cross-legged opposite me, watching silently while I drank my wine and picked at my meal with silver chopsticks.

"He must be a very trusted servant," Yuan remarked as he watched the food taster take a morsel from each dish before the delicacies were placed before me. The taster and all of my other attendants immediately retreated to the far corners of the room, behind various screens and walls to give me a semblance of privacy.

"It is a very privileged position," I pointed out. "A taster dines on the most expensive of wines and the best food in the kingdom. In return, he faces danger on my behalf."

"There is little danger if one is tasting for someone who is well-loved."

I smiled acidly at him. "While I am well-hated?"

He didn't deny it. I decided not to take offense.

"The Emperor's taster faces much more danger than mine," I said. "There is little political gain in assassinating a princess. Certainly one who has not given birth to any potential heirs."

My brother was overly protective of me. I was the one who was closest to him, after all. He didn't trust his Empress or any of his other imperial consorts. Certainly not any of our treacherous family.

The thought made me uncomfortable. Our pasts had linked Ziye and me inextricably together.

I took a sip of wine and lifted a slice of roasted duck to my lips. For the first time, I noticed how Yuan's eyes followed my every move.

"You're hungry," I realized.

Yuan shook his head.

"You haven't had anything to eat all day."

"I'm fine, Princess."

I held the slice of meat out to him, a wicked smile touching my lips. "Here."

"I'm not hungry."

Of course he would deny it. If he wanted to eat, he'd have to take it from my hands and proud Yuan would do no such thing.

"Come now." I leaned closer, waving my chopsticks toward him, taunting.

"*I'm not hungry*," he repeated firmly.

His fingers had just taken hold of my wrist when we were interrupted by the cry of an imperial messenger.

"The Emperor summons Imperial Princess Shanyin to the inner palace!"

The command echoed throughout my apartment. There was no questioning an imperial summons. I was to go immediately.

"Don't starve while I'm away," I said to Yuan with a sly look as I placed the chopsticks back onto the serving tray.

I left him then to go to my brother.

A litter was waiting for me outside as a journey from my palace to the Emperor's residence could take nearly an hour on foot. Four carriers lifted the litter onto their shoulders and began their trek through the imperial grounds while I sat inside the curtained transport, shielded from the sun.

Tension coiled along my neck and shoulders, removing

all the wonderful work Yuan had done in our bath this morning. What could my brother want?

When I reached the imperial residence, the guardsmen and servants and cronies who attended to the Emperor all kowtowed and swung aside to allow me entrance. It was well known that I was the most trusted of my brother's confidants, more so than the highly ranked ministers and eunuchs who hovered about, seeking favor and recognition.

Ziye was in his private quarters in a state of undress that was far from royal in appearance. His robe was open and his hair disheveled. I could hear the sound of weeping in the inner chamber.

"Elder Sister. I'm beginning to believe that to be Emperor is to be constantly disappointed in those around me."

He sprawled onto one of the long benches in the antechamber. Sometimes I forgot he was merely seventeen years of age. Old enough to officially rule in his own name, but prey to the whims and impulses of youth. The weeping continued on the other side of the silk screen that divided the room. I spared a glance toward the inner chamber before going to stand over Ziye.

"Is it not late for the Son of Heaven to still be in his private quarters?" I asked gently. "Is the imperial court not waiting for him?"

His black hair was unbound, falling down to his shoulders. He regarded me from behind a long section that had fallen over his eye. "So dismiss the court."

I imagined the rows of ministers and secretaries waiting

in the audience hall for his appearance, their foreheads pressed to the floor.

"Ziye—"

"You go and listen to them," he said with a shrug. "Tell them you're there on the Emperor's behalf. Their complaints make my head hurt."

He knew I would do no such thing. As a rule, I didn't involve myself in court politics. The schemes and workings would go on with or without our involvement, but Ziye as Emperor needed to at least make an effort.

I took an empty seat across from him. "What is troubling you, Brother?"

Something had put him in a foul mood and it was obvious the woman sobbing in the far corner of the room was involved.

"It's Sparrow," he said with a toss of his head. "She's become tiresome to me."

Sparrow. One of his newest concubines. I only knew the name because he'd mentioned her more than once.

"Why Ziye! She remained your favorite for nearly the entire summer," I said with a knowing smile.

Usually he found my wry humor amusing, but today he scowled. "She's become willful, abusive of my favor. Thinking she has some hold over me."

"Then be rid of her," I suggested, which brought on a fresh wail from the screen. Apparently Little Sparrow was eavesdropping on our conversation.

"Women are all the same, with their lying eyes and the stink of perfume wherever they go. Pretending to be flowers and gems and flittering birds," he spat, but then a wistful look crossed his face. "Except for you, my dearest Shanyin."

Shanyin wasn't my birth name, but the name he'd given me to indicate my status. Much like I bestowed names upon my harem. The pinnacle of femininity, the title proclaimed. The ruling lady of this imperial court.

I didn't quite like how he looked at me now, almost worshipful. My younger brother needed to find goddesses to worship and he did so repeatedly, in a beautiful face or the graceful sway of slender hips or perhaps a pretty singing voice. He would be utterly fascinated until he took her to bed and immediately learned that she was no goddess after all. Then he'd smash her to pieces like a false idol.

"If they could only be more like you, Sister."

He reached out to touch my cheek, but I stood and slipped away from the contact. "Well, let me see this disobedient concubine of yours."

I stood before the screen and stared at the vague shape behind it. My stomach sickened when I thought of what state the girl must be in. At least she wasn't too broken to make a sound.

"Come out, Little Sparrow," I called softly. "Dry your tears. Your song no longer pleases the Emperor."

Ziye didn't counter my command, but I could hear him sitting up on the bench. Gradually, the sobbing grew silent and a slender girl appeared from behind the painted silk. She was no older than fifteen herself, a frightened little thing. She had a handkerchief pressed to her lips to muffle her cries. Though the layers of her silk robe were wrapped around her, I could see the welts on the side of her neck and even over her hands where she had tried to defend herself. Perhaps that was what had enraged the Emperor; such a willful, disobedient concubine, raising her hands to him.

I took hold of the girl's chin, tilting it gently upward. Her face was streaked with tears and there was a fresh gash across her cheek. The streak of blood appeared stark against the paleness of her skin. Two large eyes darted to mine before quickly looking away.

"A pity," I declared. "She's quite pretty."

Behind me, Ziye snorted. "I thought her pretty once too, but now the sight of her disgusts me. My manhood can barely stay hard long enough to fuck her."

His cruel words brought fresh tears to Sparrow's eyes. The poor creature. Not too long ago, she had probably been certain of the Emperor's love for her and the bright future that would come with it.

"Perhaps you should give her to me, then," I suggested lightly. "So that I might educate her in the ways of men and women."

Ziye's mouth twisted into a sneer. "Aren't you occupied with your newest infatuation?"

Once again his tone took on an edge of jealousy when he spoke of Yuan. I glanced over at him, watching his expression carefully.

"He certainly is entertaining," I replied with a shrug. "But only useful for the first quarter of an hour or so. His stamina leaves something to be desired."

My brother laughed sharply and stood, finally righting his robe. "Take her. I'm interested to see if you can make any improvements."

I took my leave and strode away from the imperial apartments, leaving Sparrow to shuffle behind me. When we reached the litter, she needed assistance to climb in and I noticed how she winced when the attendant took hold of her arm.

"Show me," I commanded as soon as the curtain fell. Outside, the carriers lifted us to start the journey back to my palace.

Sparrow froze and stared at me. How did my brother ever have any interest in such a meek and shrinking creature?

"No one can see you. Show me what he did."

Slowly she turned away and let the edge of her robe slip from her shoulders. Red welts crisscrossed all along her back and shoulders. He'd taken a bamboo switch to her.

I told her she could cover up. She did so gingerly, but there was no avoiding the welts. A fresh sob escaped from her lips and she bit down hard to keep from crying.

"What happened?"

"I didn't mean any offense! You must believe me, Princess."

I let out a sigh. "I believe you, but he is the Emperor. If he takes offense then you are at fault."

I wasn't trying to be cruel, but the girl had to know that there was no understanding some of the things my brother did. And she needed to stop her damn crying as if it would gain her any sympathy from him.

"The Emperor summoned me from the women's palace in the middle of the morning," Sparrow began, her voice trembling. "By the time I arrived, it seemed his Imperial Majesty was upset about something. Nothing—nothing I did seemed to please him. The Emperor then commanded me to get on my knees and he pushed his…pushed himself into my mouth—"

"There is no need to give me all the details," I interrupted with a roll of my eyes. "What made him so angry?"

Sparrow blushed bright red. "I wasn't prepared. I could barely breathe and when he pulled out my teeth scraped onto…onto his…"

"Dragon?" I finished for her.

Not noticing my mocking tone, Sparrow nodded. "He became furious. He struck me across the face and then started beating me. I was so frightened. So humiliated."

I inspected the cut across her cheek once more where my brother's ring had marred her face. "You are fortunate the Emperor summoned me before he did any worse."

I knew my brother was often immature and impulsive. But the worst was when he was trying to prove his power. Then he transformed from a self-serving and selfish youth to a tyrant and then nothing could sway him. Certainly not a few soothing words from me, his elder sister.

"I am most grateful, Princess. I'll do anything, anything you ask of me."

I nodded, accepting her thanks without reply. There were things I could do, if I were intent on weaving an intricate scheme. I could tutor Sparrow back into my brother's good graces. Then I could have her be my eyes and ears in the women's quarters so she could pass me information about Ziye's wife. I was certain the Empress was plotting my death.

But I had swum in the infested waters of palace politics all my life. All I wanted now were simple pleasures as my reward for surviving. Wealth, comfort and beautiful men in my bed to attend to my every desire.

When we reached my palace, I summoned a physician to tend to Sparrow's wounds. I didn't see any other signs of lasting damage, but I wanted to be certain. After that, I needed to act fast. As impulsive as Ziye was, he might have already decided he wanted Little Sparrow back beneath his thumb. I left the palace to make arrangements and didn't return until evening time.

Lanterns glowed around the perimeter of my private quarters and I entered to see Sparrow curled up asleep on a raised bench in the parlor. She roused as soon as I came inside and fell to her knees.

"Princess," she greeted, pressing her forehead to the ground.

I bade her to rise from the floor and then sank down myself onto one of the seats. My head pounded from having to deal with so many unpleasant details.

"You have a decision to make, Sparrow. And you must make it tonight before the Emperor comes searching for you."

Her eyes lit up and I wondered whether it was out of anticipation or fear at the thought of seeing my brother again. I would soon know the answer.

"There is a temple at the far edge of the province where I can send you. It is a quiet place, located near a lake. You can live out the rest of your life there as a Buddhist nun. Your head will be shaved. Your days will be filled with nothing but prayer and meditation. Your food will be bland, but you will be fed. Consider that existence, a life of abstinence, rejecting all earthly pleasures. Then consider the life you have led: a lover to the Emperor, sleeping on the finest silk and dining on meat with every meal. But know this." I regarded her with the most serious expression I could conjure. "You might be able to return to a life of luxury as an imperial concubine and even hope to be elevated in rank should you give birth to a son. But it is inevitable that one day you will displease the Emperor again, through no fault of your own. And he will be angry enough this time to really hurt you. Perhaps even kill you. He may regret it later. He may even finally profess his love, but only your spirit will hear it."

I didn't have long to wait for an answer. "The temple," Sparrow said. "If the Emperor won't ever find me there, then that is where I wish to be."

"I will make certain that he doesn't."

Sparrow bowed, kowtowing to me three times to display how grateful she was. Then I sent her off with an armed escort to take her away from the palace and to her new life.

By then I was tired, too tired to bother summoning any of my harem to me. As I wove around the screen into my sleeping chamber, I was startled to see Yuan still there. He'd moved off of the bed and was seated with his back against the wall, arms folded as he regarded me curiously.

I blinked at him. "You're still here."

Yuan rose to come toward me. "I was never dismissed."

He had waited here all this time. I glanced at the bed. The tray of food was exactly as I'd left it, untouched.

"Then you heard everything." My chest tightened. I didn't want anyone seeing me like this, my nerves strained and pulled thin.

"Enough to figure out the story. How exactly do you plan to keep the Emperor from reclaiming his concubine?"

"Easy." I waved my hand casually, as if shooing away a fly. "I will tell him of the dreams that plagued her. Then I'll tell him how the court astrologer declared those dreams were visions and that Sparrow was fated to become a nun. It was her destiny—no wonder she couldn't properly satisfy him in bed. My brother has always been very superstitious."

"And you are not," Yuan observed.

"It's all fable to me, but it occasionally serves my purpose."

"A heretic, then."

I shrugged away the insult. "If I had known you were here, I could have given Little Sparrow to you to corrupt instead. With your vast experience in the ways of love, you would have been the perfect tutor."

I meant to rile him, but I was so exhausted that the

taunt came out flat. Resigned, I waved him away, but Yuan remained where he was.

"You gave her a choice," he remarked. "And moved mountains to do so."

"Hardly mountains."

"Why?"

"No one questions me," I said exasperated, but Yuan waited for an answer.

"It was my mood today. If it were yesterday or tomorrow, who knows what might have happened?" I went to lay down upon my bed, still fully clothed. "Now, are you going to stay and strip me naked, or will I see you again tomorrow?"

His gaze lingered on me for a second before he bowed and took his leave.

CHAPTER THREE

I am beginning to adore the way Yuan appears each morning. His robe is impeccable, his long hair tied back. He stands with his shoulders straight and his jaw set, awaiting whatever whim I might have. He's foregone with the bowing and the customary kowtows. I should probably reprimand him for that, but I do love the way he stands there waiting for me. He's stiff, like a granite statue. His expression remains blank as if the night has cleansed him all of the intimacies and vulgarities of the previous day.

How will he appear when he wakes up in my bed, with no chance to wash away such wrongs?

"I want to see what you look like when you come," I told him. I hadn't thought of it until that moment, seeing him standing so rigid and controlled before me.

Yuan didn't flinch when I stood to approach him, but I saw how hard he fought against the impulse. I opened his robe for him while he continued to stand still, staring beyond me rather than at me.

"It is only fair." I pushed the edge of the cloth aside and then worked the tunic beneath loose to expose the plane of his chest. He would be such a pleasure to explore with my hands, but there would be time for that later. "You have seen me at my most vulnerable, after all."

His eyes had been fixed onto me while he brought me to climax. No matter how he denied it, the sight had made him hard. I wondered if he was hard now.

I met his gaze and for a moment I saw something flicker beneath the cold stare. It was the same look I'd seen last night when he'd asked me all those meddlesome questions. I realized that the moment I'd felt most vulnerable before him wasn't when I was writhing naked in my bed. It was when I'd been fully clothed and Yuan had seen inside me.

Looking away, I reached for his trousers. My hand paused before undoing the ties. "Shall I perform the act or shall I call one of the maidservants?"

I tilted my head up. From there I could see the sculpted angles of his face. His throat worked as he swallowed. "You," he said finally, his voice hoarse.

I had been hoping that would be his answer. Anticipation warmed my skin and pulled my nipples into peaks. "So you don't despise me after all."

He finally looked down to meet my eyes. "The Princess has already seen my body. I don't wish to corrupt anyone else."

My laughter rang throughout the parlor. With my hand planted against his chest, I pushed him back, directing him onto one of the benches in the sitting area. It had a wide seat, long enough for me to recline, but I left Yuan sitting in the center of it. I took the spot next to him, my body curving over his while he remained wooden beside me.

I raised myself to whisper in his ear, my breasts pressing against his shoulder. "Proud and upstanding Yuan, afraid of corrupting young maidens with his naked body."

A shudder went through him. I wanted to sink my teeth into his neck and taste the salt of his skin. Instead I kissed him, very softly, just below his ear. I don't think he liked it. If he were a horse, he would have flicked his ear at me in annoyance, but I didn't care. I was enjoying myself too much.

As I reached into his lap, I had a full view of his thighs. They were well-muscled, like the rest of him. Between them, I could see a bulge forming as his body responded to having a woman so close.

Instead of untying the trousers, I cupped my hand between his legs and heard a hiss of breath as his sex stirred against my fingers.

"I know what you're thinking," I murmured against his ear in a sing-song. "You're telling yourself that this means nothing. That your body is responding, but your mind, your pure and honorable mind, is unmoved."

I pressed the heel of my hand downward and rubbed slowly. Yuan clenched his hands into fists by his side but his organ swelled beneath my touch, straining upward to seek release. I undid his trousers quickly and his hips lifted to accommodate me when I pushed the material down over them.

He sat now with his robe parted and trousers lowered, sex exposed. Otherwise, he remained fully clothed. He appeared more vulnerable this way; his clothes in disarray, clinging desperately onto the vestiges of civility.

I filled my hands with him. He wasn't as large as the most well-endowed of my harem, but he wasn't smaller by much. His organ was long and thick and perfectly formed. The blunt head had darkened in color like a ripe plum. I longed to swirl the tip of my tongue over it, but I also wanted to watch his face as he released. I moved my thumb in a small circle over the tip, sliding through the bead of moisture that gathered there.

"Yin is yin and yang is yang," I said.

His flesh tightened even further in my grasp. I think he liked it when I spoke to him even though he was gritting his teeth now, fighting an invisible foe. I wanted him to try to hold back. It would make the torture all the more exquisite.

Lightly, I stroked my hand down the length of him while I watched his face. He shook his head sharply, denial in every inch of his body except for the part I had in hand. Meanwhile his cock twitched to seek out my touch. I rewarded it with another stroke, firmer this time.

So that was how he liked it. Hard. His hips churned as he forced himself back against the seat. Why fight so hard? It was only release. Orgasm. As natural and necessary as breathing.

I couldn't take my eyes off of him. Selfishly, I dragged my hand along his cock twice more, purposefully not providing enough pressure to take him to his peak. I loved watching how he burned.

By now, he was so hard that it must have pained him.

His expression was caught between agony and ecstasy and his breathing was shallow, quick and uneven. He gasped when I squeezed him harder. The skin of his shaft was velvet smooth and pulsing with life as his heartbeat increased.

"There are men who feel they lose something of themselves when they surrender to a woman like this. Spilling their seed into the cold, empty air. It doesn't have to be that way." My hand never stopped moving. His entire body was drawn tight like a bowstring, every muscle vibrating for release. I had found a rhythm that suited him.

I was fascinated by the sight of Yuan struggling beside me. His body was begging for me even if he would never admit it. If I poured oil over him, he would slide hard and fast through my hands. It wouldn't take long to give him the release his body so desperately needed. If I let him into my mouth, he might go even faster with my lips and tongue urging him to new heights. But I wanted to watch him as he lost himself.

What I really wanted was for him to take me with him. I could feel my own wetness between my legs, my body readying itself for a man. Yuan was fiercely beautiful as he writhed beside me and my body was not used to being denied.

"It would be so good," I whispered to him. "You know it would be."

I pressed my lips against Yuan's bare collarbone and his cock jumped. He liked it when I touched him and not only with my hands on his cock.

"It would be so easy," I urged. I was no longer taunting him. I no longer had the will. If I straddled him now and lowered myself onto him, he would penetrate me with hardly any effort at all. I was swollen and empty, needing him to fill me.

"No."

He insisted on gritting out his denial. A moment later, his muscles locked and his seed erupted out onto his lap, spilling hot over my hand in the process. His hips jerked in a sporadic rhythm which continued even when his peak had come and gone.

At the last moment, before he'd come, his eyes had squeezed shut and his head had fallen back. It was the moment he knew his release was inevitable and had surrendered to it. It was also a moment of agonizing beauty. The sight of him was branded into my memory.

His sex gradually softened, desire spent. When I removed my hand, he immediately turned away.

"Let me—" His voice came out ragged and he had to start again. "Let me clean myself."

I directed him to a basin of water in the corner, dipping a cloth so I could wash my hand before returning to the center of the room. Yuan worked quickly, his back turned to me. I granted him this silence.

I felt no particular triumph in seeing him unmanned. It was merely for my own selfish pleasure. I was still flushed from the feel of his powerful body shuddering against mine. If only he could have been on top of me, his organ pushed deep inside. I would have wrapped my legs around his hips to absorb every last thrust. As it was, I was left hungry, the lips of my sex swollen and unfulfilled.

"It's just sex," I said lightly. "Neither sacred, nor profane."

He didn't answer.

"There is no need for shame."

"I'm not ashamed by what happens between a man and a woman," he replied, still turned away. His tone was cold.

Heat rose up the back of my neck. "Then it's me you find objectionable."

Once again, Yuan fell silent. He soothed a hand over the front of his robe and then moved to the window to stare out into the garden.

"Answer me!"

He turned only partway, refusing to face me directly. "I do not wish to have my tongue cut out."

I should have called in my guards to drag Yuan outside and carry out my threat. Instead I wanted him to drag me to the floor and take me then and there. In anger, if that was what he needed. I imagined how that anger would fuel his passion, pushing him deeper and harder into me.

But Yuan composed himself quickly. By the time he was following me obediently to the polo grounds, the flush was gone from his face and his expression was as dispassionate as ever. I could almost believe he was unaffected by me, but he froze whenever I "inadvertently" brushed against him. He tried to keep his distance as much as possible. Yet when my fingertips grazed over his knuckles, his breath stuttered.

It was only a matter of time, I told myself, grinning inwardly. I had seven more days.

The men of my harem had assembled for a polo match. They had been separated into two teams and rode astride horses from the Emperor's stable. Those who remained on foot served as handlers.

"This should be very entertaining. I promised the winning team a special reward," I explained with a coy glance over my shoulder.

Yuan followed behind me and had to dodge away from the sweep of my parasol as I turned. Without warning, he reached out and took the bamboo handle from me. He held the parasol overhead, shielding me from the sun as we continued toward the playing field. The action brought him closer to my side. Ah, gallantry.

An awning had been set up on the grass with seats beneath it fashioned from rattan. I took a seat in the shade with Yuan at my side, pressed close by the width of the bench. We were surrounded by my retinue of attendants and bodyguards, but the polo match was purely for my entertainment.

The players assembled in a row before me to bow and pay their respects. I hadn't called any one of them to my bed last night, which always made them particularly competitive. There was more than one sharp glance directed at Yuan.

"You are fortunate this is not an archery match," I

teased, squeezing his arm.

Surprisingly, Yuan didn't stiffen or draw away from the touch. It made me feel outright affectionate toward him. And why shouldn't I be feeling fond? The sun was shining. I was the most powerful woman in the empire and surrounded by my doting harem as well as one stubborn, challenging quarry who didn't despise me nearly as much as he claimed.

"Little do they realize they have no need to be jealous," I went on. "You've never had me beneath you whereas every one of them has taken me at least once a month. Sometimes twice," I added, staring at that granite profile.

Yuan folded his arms over his chest. "We're surrounded by others."

"I'm always surrounded," I replied, unfazed. "The concubines think I have a new favorite. An outsider who isn't one of them. It must make them furious."

He glanced at me and then away. I loved how agitated I made him. "It's dangerous to play a man's passions against him," he warned gruffly.

"There is always one favorite or another. They are quite accustomed to it."

"I don't wish to be called a favorite."

"I did no such thing," I countered sweetly. Then I leaned close, close enough my lips could almost graze his ear. "We haven't even kissed, my darling."

The polo match had started with the team in green making a drive toward the opposite field. Yuan made a show of watching the exchange of the ball from one player to the next. I settled back in my seat, deciding to behave for a little while at least.

"No man would tolerate his woman being possessed by someone else," Yuan said, staring directly ahead.

I was surprised to hear him speak. It was the first time he had initiated conversation.

"They are just slaves," I dismissed. "I don't belong to them. They belong to me."

A sense of pride filled me as I scanned the field. Thirty able-bodied young men, beautiful in face and form and mine to command. The captain of the yellow team raised his stick and swung hard, driving the ball away from his goal and back into enemy territory. He looked to the awning and caught my eye. I smiled back at him with an encouraging nod. Yao, handsome by name and by face. He shot a poisoned glance at Yuan before galloping down the field.

"That is not how they think of it," Yuan said, his point made.

I knew he was right in part. These men were my concubines, but once in a while, they held a princess in their arms and made her cry out in pleasure. When I surrendered to any one of them, he became prince for a night.

But Yuan wasn't a slave. He was an aristocrat with a good name who held rank within the court.

"Would you feel differently if you were the only man in my bed?"

A cheer rose from the yellow sashes which saved Yuan

from having to answer immediately.

"Nothing would change between us, Princess," he answered.

He was insufferable. He was also as unmoving as the mountains and it made me burn for him all the more.

"You do realize the sooner I have you, the sooner I'll tire of you."

I don't know if I said it for his sake or mine. One part of me hated having to negotiate at all, but the other part of me was dying to have him. The same part of me that was getting frustrated with all the toying and teasing.

"How about this proposal? We'll gather the clouds and the rain tonight until the lanterns burn out and then I'll free you in the morning?"

I pressed against his side as I spoke, soft curves against hard angles. My hand slid over his knee suggestively. His thighs were hard beneath my palm.

He raised an eyebrow at me skeptically. I was surprised to see his lips twitch with amusement. "The clouds and the rain?"

"I thought such poetic imagery would appeal to your prudish nature," I said with a smile. Then I pressed closer, my arms circling his neck. "Fuck me," I said into his ear, my voice low so that only he could hear. "Fuck me all night and I'll let you go."

I regretted the offer the moment I made it. I had been promised ten days and I didn't want to let him go, but my stomach also fluttered with the thought that he might accept. That would mean I could have him tonight in every way I had imagined. I didn't think he would give in to me yet, but it was possible. He hadn't drawn away from me. We were practically entwined upon the bench.

The polo match continued before us, but I hardly cared what was happening. My focus was completely on Yuan, whose pulse had quickened when I told him to fuck me.

"You'll likely be a disappointment," I goaded silkily.

A fierce light sparked in his eyes. That barb certainly got his attention. No man could tolerate his woman in the embrace of another, and no man would allow his manhood to be challenged without taking up arms.

He took hold of me with his hands on either side of my hips. The movement caught me by surprise and I thought he meant to push me away, but his grip tightened on me, his thumbs pressing into the indent of my waist.

His gaze smoldered hot enough to burn me to ashes, but that touch…that touch told me things. It told me exactly how he would hold me down, how he would command my body as he pushed into me. It also told me how I would melt beneath him until there was nothing left of me but heat and a deep, endless spiral to oblivion.

I almost wished he would be a disappointment in the end. He had become idealized in my mind, an incredible lover who frightened me as much as he enticed me. Yuan would take me a hundred different ways until I fainted from the pleasure, unable to take any more. If he were half that good, I would be the one enslaved. I had already revealed more of myself to him than any of my lovers.

A thundering sound filled my ears and I thought it was

the rush of blood through my head, but the pounding grew louder. I looked up to see one of the horses rampaging toward us. His rider was struggling to pull back on the reins.

Screams shattered the air as my entourage scattered. The great steed filled my vision, his hooves lifting until he reared up on his hind legs. His great eye seemed to fix onto me and my limbs turned to stone. A scream stuck in my throat as the hooves came crashing down.

Rough hands grabbed me. I could hear my silk robe tearing as I was thrown onto the grass. Stunned, I turned my head to see Yuan standing between me and the enraged animal. From where I lay, Yuan towered over me, but the horse was even more massive. His hooves hovered dangerously close to Yuan's head.

Yuan held out his hands, palm out. Rather than backing away, he moved toward the steed. I dug my hands into the grass, trying to drag myself up. He would be crushed!

The horse's front legs came plummeting down, but Yuan stepped smoothly out of the way, taking position by the animal's shoulder. Yuan took hold of the reins and the horse made an agitated sound, shaking his head. Shortly after, the creature seemed to calm down. By then, the stable hands came forward to take command of the horse.

"We shall have the beast punished, Princess!" the head groomsman promised.

"Better to punish the rider," Yuan growled. "And all of you who were responsible for handling the horses."

The groomsman shrank back. Handsome Yao had been

the rider. He had been unseated and remained sprawled in the grass on his hands and knees, his face pale. Whether he was shaken from being thrown or afraid of retribution from me, I couldn't tell. I was still shaken myself. My arms and legs couldn't seem to work. When I tried to stand up, I staggered back onto the ground.

Several of the men had dismounted to rush toward me, but Yuan reached me first. His arm closed around my waist to lift me to my feet. I clung to him, not caring who saw me in my moment of weakness. Not caring was one of the privileges of being princess.

As Yuan barked orders to the attendants, I saw how he was undeniably an aristocrat. Despite how I treated him, he was not a servant to be overlooked or ignored. My attendants must have realized this as well as they scurried to do his bidding.

My palanquin was brought to transport me back to my quarters. When the attendants moved to lift me from the carriage, I pointed to Yuan who had accompanied the procession the entire way.

"You," I insisted.

Without batting an eye, he bent to lift me, carrying me in his arms to my bedchamber. With each step, my heart beat faster. He was the one who had pulled me out of danger. He had put his person between me and a mindless beast, a creature who could not be negotiated with.

He laid me down onto my bed and methodically began to check me for injuries. His capable hands massaged along my arms, my ankles, testing for broken bones I assumed.

"You could just ask if I'm hurt," I said, surprised at how violently I was still shaking.

"You're in shock," he said impatiently, holding me still when I tried to move. "You wouldn't be able to tell."

His head remained bent as he tested the joint of my knee. Warmth pooled low in my belly, melting away the numbness that had set in. I liked how his hands felt on me when he touched me of his own free will. I liked it very much.

He shifted up alongside me and skimmed his palms upward over my ribs. My chest heaved with each breath and my heart felt as if it would burst out of my chest. His inspection stopped short of my breasts, his fingertips just grazing the soft skin underneath.

Oh, I was not wide-eyed and innocent enough to believe all of this was unintentional. Curling my fingers into the front of his robe, I dragged him to me, my mouth pressing against his in a sigh of breath.

His lips were yielding, warm; but only for a moment. Yuan wouldn't allow my kiss for any longer than the blink of an eye.

"I would have done the same for anyone," he insisted after pulling away.

I didn't push any further. The fleeting touch of his mouth was enough to sustain me for the day, which was odd, considering it sometimes took the earnest efforts of three men for me to find any sense of satisfaction.

That night I ordered Yuan relocated to one of the chambers nearest to me. I didn't want to have to wait for him to answer my summons every morning. Not when my time with him was growing short.

CHAPTER FOUR

My concubines secured Yuan's arms the moment he set foot in my bedchamber. They shoved him toward the bed while I finished my morning tea in the corner.

Yuan fought them, as I knew he would, but my lovers were not like the pale and fleshy eunuchs who attended to the Emperor. They were tall and strong, as strong as Yuan was. Five of them were more than enough to subdue him and strip away his clothing while he flailed and kicked.

"Shanyin!"

No title. No honorific attached to my name. He could be punished for that alone, but being overpowered by my men was likely punishment enough. I watched while they used long strips of silk to tie his arms and legs to the posts of the bed. I had put much thought into the design of this legendary bed, as you can see.

When they were done, Yuan lay completely naked at the head of the bed with arms and legs stretched wide. I appreciated the flex of his muscles as he continued to struggle. He was masculine and well-formed and my stomach fluttered just looking at him. Even tied down, he didn't appear helpless.

The men had been rougher with him than I had

anticipated. Tai Jin stood back and looked down at Yuan with an air of satisfaction. Then my former favorite looked to me expectantly. A few mornings ago, Yuan had stood by the bed while Tai and his partner had pleasured me at the same time. The concubine probably thought I would require his services now, but he was mistaken. He would be a distraction and I wanted to focus on one man alone.

With a flick of my hand, I sent the concubines away. A look of relief flashed over Yuan's face, but it was quickly replaced with a combination of fear and desire. I knew both well.

"Princess, this is unnecessary." He tugged at the silken ties. There was enough slack in the bonds to make some movement possible, but he was held securely in place and at my mercy.

"Oh, it is necessary, darling." I loosened my sash to let my robe slip from my shoulders.

Silk pooled on the floor at my feet. I stepped over it to stalk toward the bed. Yuan's eyes couldn't help but roam over me, darkening as they lingered. For the first time, we were both disrobed and naked at the same time. There was no hiding how my breasts were swollen and heavy, the nipples dark and peaked. And there was no hiding how his cock thickened as I came near.

There was no coyness or flirtation in my approach. I climbed onto the bed and straddled his hips, my thighs spreading wide to settle down onto the bed. The tip of his sex nestled against my slit and Yuan gritted his teeth as I slid myself back and forth over the smooth head of his cock, letting him know I was wet and that I was ready for him.

I lowered my hands to his shoulders to press him down into the pallet. "You need to be held down, don't you? You need to say that you don't want this."

"I don't—"

I silenced him with my mouth over his. The fight drained from him the moment our lips met and he returned the kiss with the same hunger as I. His tongue slid inside my mouth; the mere touch of lips and mingling of our breath not enough after how long we'd waited.

He tasted like tea with a spicy tang of cloves. My stomach fluttered and my body liquefied as the kiss grew deeper.

With a groan, he broke away. "My hands," he growled.

It wasn't a plea. He would never beg me, but I wanted him to. I wanted it very much.

I shook my head and captured his mouth again, letting my hands roam down his shoulders to his chest. The flat of his stomach. He tensed and bucked as I reached his thighs, but the silk held him fast.

He moaned something incoherently. Whatever it was, the words were cut short when he exhaled sharply. I had taken hold of his manhood, gripping him gently as if he were fragile. I knew he wasn't. I wasn't the only one who appreciated a rough touch.

"I want you to tell me yes." My tone was hard, but my hand soft as I stroked him from tip to root. "Your body is already telling me everything I need to know, but I want to hear it."

He shook his head and his eyes squeezed shut. I took hold of his bottom lip between my teeth and bit gently.

"*Yes*," I insisted against his mouth.

It was the sentiment in my own heart. As my hips moved restlessly over his sex, my body grew more damp and swollen. Hard over soft. I pressed my mound down over him, shifting to find the right angle of my hips.

Yuan's hands clenched into fists over his head. The silk was pulled taut and his body had nearly raised off the bed in an effort to escape. He was not accustomed to being used in such a way, but he still wanted it. I could tell by the way his organ hardened even more between my thighs. If I guided him to my entrance and pushed forward, he would slide inside me. The thought made my knees week.

"Tell me to do it," I said, breathless.

"No," he insisted. "Never."

Insufferable man. I was caught in my promise to not force myself upon him. I realized then that even if I hadn't made that promise, I would still be caught in a trap. I didn't want to take, I wanted to be taken. Hard and repeatedly. I wanted to be drained of all desire and fucked until there was nothing left inside me but him.

I climbed up along his body, letting him feel me sliding over him until my nipple was at the level of his mouth. Yuan needed no instruction here. The moment the soft curve of my breast touched him, he knew what I wanted. His mouth opened and clamped hot over my breast, making my toes curl in response. Before I could find my breath, the tip of his tongue slid back and forth over my nipple. Gently at first and then harder as I squirmed against him. A deep, spiraling sensation built in my womb, threatening to take me over. I was possessed by the need to climax and by the need for him to bring me there. Him. The only man who had ever dared to refuse me.

I fed my other breast into his mouth and he sucked me greedily. Beneath me, his body strained upward. There was no doubt what he wanted. What we both wanted.

"Now," I moaned, fitting my hips to his. His stiff organ was trapped between our bodies and I could feel the heat radiating from his skin.

"Untie me," he rasped.

So he could use his hands to escape? "Never."

I fisted my hands into his dark hair, pulling back hard enough for him to exhale sharply. His organ swelled and I shifted my thighs so the tip of it pressed against my sex. I was slick, aching and ready for him and I knew he could feel it because he stopped breathing altogether.

"This is what you want," I panted. I circled my hips, bathing the head of his cock in my fluids. The sensation was incredible, like nothing else I'd known. And it was only the beginning.

But Yuan shook his head. The lying bastard!

I cried out in frustration, a sob lodging in my throat. It would be so easy to reach down and guide his manhood into me. I would lower myself onto him, bit by glorious bit. Savor and torture him for every moment he'd made me wait.

Yuan's head was thrown back and his face caught in a mask of exquisite agony. If I rode him until we both climaxed, he'd say I'd claimed his body while his mind rebelled.

I raked my nails over his torso and his eyes flew open. "Tell me," I demanded.

He shook his head. "I can't. I won't."

I bit him then, sprawling over him to sink my teeth into his shoulder, making him cry out. I couldn't take him, not the way I wanted to. This was our game, our covenant, but my body wanted his so badly. I wanted him so much that taking merely pleasure from him was not enough. I wanted his will, his pain. And I wanted to know what this mysterious force was that kept him from me.

I ground my hips into him, rubbing my throbbing sex over his cock. A waste, my soul lamented. But it didn't matter. The sensation was enough to make my insides tighten. Desperately, I repeated the motion, closing my eyes at the lurid pleasure of it. I was mindless now, sliding his cock between my slick folds. Inelegant. I didn't care.

My back arched to press our bodies one precious breath closer. Below me, Yuan groaned, full of both ecstasy and frustration. He could only feel me sliding over his head and part of his shaft. The rest of his manhood was sorely neglected. His choice.

His arms strained against the silk bonds and his face was a grimace of denial and unwanted pleasure. I closed my eyes while my hips circled with abandon. I didn't want to see his expression. I only wanted to concentrate on how his flesh felt against mine. Hard against soft and heat, so much heat.

Yuan choked out something. It sounded like my name, but he would never admit it. A moment later, a hot splash of fluid coated my belly. Apparently my ministrations were enough to bring him to climax after all. He hissed as I continued to grind. I was too greedy, mindful only of my own needs to stop.

Suddenly, the muscles of my back seized. My insides clenched tight and bright spots swam beneath my eyelids. I was there, shuddering and lost in orgasm.

When I could move again, I opened my eyes to see Yuan looking up at me. His expression was unreadable. Unapologetically, I sank into the crook of his arm, resting my head against his shoulder. He had no choice but to let me, tied down as he was.

"Bastard," I accused, suddenly sleepy.

There were easier, more satisfying ways to achieve release and I was still angry at him for denying me.

"Untie me," he rasped.

His heart was still pounding and his skin damp with sweat. Mine was as well. I could see where my nails had left scratches across his chest. I traced one red line with the tip of my finger and ignored his request.

No man could possess such restraint. It had to be soon. Six days was more than enough time to tempt a man who was already not quite unwilling. *Soon*, I promised myself silently. And it would feel like nothing else I'd ever experienced. My mouth went dry imagining the moment I would finally have him inside me.

I didn't release Yuan until my pulse was no longer racing and the heat from my climax had faded.

CHAPTER FIVE

"Look, Elder Sister. I have a gift for you."

The hairs on the back of my neck stood on end as my brother gestured for the doors to be opened. We were standing before the grand banquet hall, but there was no feast laid out today. In the center of the floor were three iron cages. A lone figure crouched in each one, still dressed in court attire.

My stomach sickened. Ziye had locked up our uncles like animals.

I tried to be as soothing as possible. "Imperial Majesty—"

"The traitor He Mai wouldn't reveal who his co-conspirators were, but it has to be one of these pigs," Ziye said, running a bamboo switch against the iron bars.

Somehow, I had managed to forget that unpleasantness in the assembly hall. My head started to pound as I tried to figure out what to say. "As satisfying as it may seem, we cannot lock up everyone who displeases us—"

"Don't you remember how they imprisoned us?" Ziye interrupted, his voice cracking. "They threatened to have us killed, Shanyin."

He was in no mood for lectures from me or anyone else.

There was a petulant whine to his tone that would have made him seem childish, if I didn't realize how dangerous his tantrums could be.

I bowed my head. "I remember."

He broke out into a grin. "Now we have imprisoned them. Traitorous dogs."

"Have mercy, Son of Heaven!" the oldest uncle begged while his hands grasped the bars.

Ziye lashed out at the exposed fingers with his switch and he fell back. The other two echoed his entreaty and I could see how much Ziye enjoyed seeing them grovel, which meant he wouldn't release them any time soon.

"Don't they look like pigs in there?" Ziye asked gleefully. "Fat and useless. Which one shall we slaughter first?"

"Don't be foolish!" I hissed.

My brother's eyes flashed at me and I realized I'd made a mistake reprimanding him in front of his enemies.

"The uncles aren't worth the trouble," I amended. "Let them remain in cages for your amusement. Then strip them of their rank and confiscate their holdings."

His eyes gleamed as he nodded. "Yes, a good thought. Pigs cannot hold rank."

The uncles tried to meet my eyes, silently begging. They hoped I would be more merciful than my brother, but when Ziye was in a mood like this, no one could sway him. I fled from the inner palace as fast as I could.

It took the rest of the day to gather the required bodyguards and maidservants and eunuchs to journey out from the palace. I sent a message to the Emperor that my elements were misaligned and my *qi* was out of balance. I needed a trip to the hot springs to soak in the curative waters.

I didn't wait for a reply. Even though it was already dark outside I gave the order for the caravan to move out. I couldn't bear to remain in the palace for another minute.

"You'll have us travel through the night?" Yuan questioned.

He alone accompanied me in my palanquin while the concubines of my harem had been left behind.

"The servants have lanterns to light their way," I replied.

The face he made indicated that my answer was somehow inadequate. That was the danger of showing too much continuous favor to one man. He began to take liberties.

Though the rest of the entourage would remain awake late into the night, the litter was large enough for Yuan and me to lie down and sleep whenever we wished. Not that I had any plans to sleep just yet.

I reclined back onto the pillows while the litter swayed beneath us. "Come here."

I wondered if he would defy me, but he came willingly. Yuan remained on his knees, but somehow didn't appear to be kneeling before me, even from that position. He wore a plain robe, dyed in the deep blue-black color of midnight. The quality of it was evident in the fineness of the material and workmanship rather than any adornment. He had ceased dressing in court attire or any other clothing denoting rank since being sent to me, but he certainly didn't look like a slave.

With a lazy hand, I reached for his belt. Inside, my belly curled tight with anticipation, but I didn't want Yuan to think he had any hold over me. Even though I'd forsaken all of my other lovers to keep only him by my side.

At the last moment, he lowered his hand over mine. "Allow me."

His voice was deep, thick with desire, and it sent a small thrill down my spine. Gently he drew my hand aside and laid it beside my head on the pillow. For a moment, my wrist was pinned while he hovered over me, large and imposing. I could barely breathe.

He removed my robe and undergarments and laid me back completely naked against the pillows. I wondered if Yuan had had a change of heart about resisting my advances, but he remained fully clothed while I was exposed.

Just outside, the carriers bore the litter at a steady pace. The caravan continued toward the hot springs, oblivious to what was transpiring inside the curtain. Or perhaps not completely oblivious. I was the immoral and lascivious Princess Shanyin. Rather than being embarrassed at the prospect of being discovered, it excited me all the more. What wicked things did Yuan intend to do to me? I couldn't wait to find out.

Reaching into his sleeve, he took out a small porcelain

bottle painted with orchids. It was the perfumed oil I produced myself from the flowers in my garden. Had Yuan planned for this? My heart beat faster, and through no will of my own my shoulders fell back, lifting my breasts as if in offering.

Yuan's look was one of determination, a look I knew well. He poured a tiny pool of oil into his hand. I lay transfixed as he rubbed his palms together, spreading and warming the fragrant liquid. His first touch was at my waist as he'd done not too long ago after rescuing me from the polo field. For a moment, his broad hands did nothing but hold me, molding and framing my hips. My belly fluttered as his oiled palms slid along my ribcage, thumbs stroking over my midsection on an inevitable path.

He reached my breasts and I pushed myself into his hands, shuddering when he stroked his thumbs directly over the hard points of my nipples. A sharply pleasurable sensation traveled from his fingers down to my sex and I moaned, not caring if the servants could hear me from outside.

But Yuan didn't linger over my breasts like I wanted him to. His hands continued on their path up to my shoulders and then my neck, teasing and working at the knots there. I was torn between directing him toward the places I wanted most to be touched, and enjoying each new sensation along with the mystery of not knowing what would come next. As skilled as my harem was at bringing me to climax, they had become routine in their attentions. Cannily efficient at reading my moods and knowing how to satisfy me in the quickest way possible.

Yuan was a riddle. I never knew what would happen between us. I didn't know if he would ever give me what I truly wanted. Each time I reached a new height of sexual pleasure with him, he held something back to taunt me that there was more, so much more to come.

His hands now roamed over my entire body, paying loving attention to parts that were often neglected. My ears, elbows, wrists. There wasn't an inch of me that was undeserving, that wasn't an object of desire.

He applied more oil when he reached my legs. As he drew broad circles over my thighs, they parted of their own accord. I could feel the wetness filmed over the lips of my sex as I opened myself. I imagined the oil combining with my fluids when his clever fingers finally found their target.

But my sex wasn't his destination. He stroked lower, down my legs, to take hold of my feet. I would have groaned with frustration if the feel of his strong hands massaging my toes wasn't a thing of pure luxury. His thumbs pressed into my soles and I thought I might come just from that.

When he turned me onto my stomach I moved willingly, my body limp. There he seemed to hesitate, perhaps to gather more oil, before the exploration continued. His touch was firmer on my back side. Maybe he had become more confident. Maybe it was because I couldn't see him, he no longer had to look at my face...I didn't want to question it.

As Yuan's hands rubbed over my back, the sensual

massage was no longer enough. He had awakened every pulse point and nerve ending on my body and I was primed and ready. I had been relaxed and compliant before, but now my muscles were tense and waiting. My hips churned against the pillows underneath me, demanding he finish what he started.

Just then, I felt Yuan's body lower over mine to plant a kiss onto the small of my back. Then he stretched his length over me, placing another kiss on my bare shoulder before reaching the crook of my neck where he laid his head against mine.

Then, with his weight pinning me from head to toe, I felt him slide his fingers into me. I gasped. His fingers were long and I was so slick and swollen the penetration felt endless.

The position was intimate and yet it wasn't. I was held beneath him, every writhe and twist of my body captured against his hard form, but I couldn't see him. Yet he was inexorably present. Surrounding me. His fingers were working me steadily toward orgasm as I panted, helpless.

His breath teased against my ear. "I can pleasure you, Princess. In all the ways there are to pleasure a woman," he offered.

Except that one final act.

I wanted to argue with him but my body was caught in an upward spiral. Any thought of protest fled away when his thumb curved to touch the apex of my sex. That tiny bud where the entirety of my being became centered. He flicked lightly over it, teasing the very tip and sending indescribable sensations to every part of my body. My toes curled and my hips bucked against him.

Yuan didn't completely deny himself. The hardness of his cock pressed against the cleft of my buttocks, grinding downward. The thumb over my soft pearl was replaced by his finger which worked me with a feather-light touch, faster and faster until I was sobbing.

I wanted his hard cock inside me so badly, but I would take this. I would take this.

I bit into the corner of a pillow as I came. It wasn't enough to muffle my cries completely and I whimpered as Yuan's hand slowed but did not stop. He circled my flesh gently now, soothingly, absorbing the tremors of my body against his.

"Again," he murmured against my ear, a command that allowed no room for denial. Gradually Yuan increased the tempo of his fingers, working me to another climax. I gritted my teeth as the tide crashed over me once more, not as sharp as the first time, but more prolonged.

My inner muscles clenched around his fingers, spasming without rhythm. He'd brought me twice to the peak, one orgasm immediately after the other, yet something kept me from being fully swept away. His insistence on taking care of my pleasure was only a ploy. A strategy on his part to maintain control.

I rolled over and reached beneath his robe. My hands closed around his erect member, squeezing hard enough to make him groan. He didn't retreat, but after one long stroke, all the pleasure he would allow himself, Yuan once again closed his hand over mine to stop me.

"She must be very beautiful for you to keep yourself for her," I challenged.

A ripple of tension traveled through him. He said nothing.

"I suppose I never give any thought to luring a man with my appearance," I went on. "With my concubines, it doesn't matter if I'm pleasing to the eye. I command and they obey."

"I've always thought you were beautiful," Yuan interjected. "That isn't the issue."

I waited for him to add something about how the prettiest of flowers were the most poisonous or how beauty was just a façade, a thin shell painted over a rotted center, but he didn't say any such thing.

"You have scars," he said instead, causing me to blink at him, not comprehending. "The scars all along your back," Yuan explained with his jaw tight.

"Those? Those are hardly worth mentioning," I replied airily. At the same time I reached for the robe crumpled beneath me and pulled it over my shoulders.

I hardly thought of those marks anymore. As I told him, it didn't matter what I looked like to my harem of lovers.

"Someone hurt you."

I was surprised he actually appeared angry.

"Don't you know?" I affected a laugh that felt thin even to my ears. "Such marks are nothing but souvenirs from a lover's game. You have a few on you from yesterday morning, if I recall."

When I tried to turn away he stopped me. "Those are merely scratches. Nothing that would leave a scar. Or so many."

I forced a smile. "My chivalrous and honorable protector. Don't you know that some games are played harder than others?"

The corners of his mouth turned downward, far from satisfied with my answer. "Just a game?" he echoed in disbelief.

I preferred the familiar look of disdain creeping back into his eyes. It was better than protectiveness or pity. Yuan refused to stick his cock into me, yet he insisted on prying into my secrets.

"Yes," I told him, averting my eyes. "Everything is merely one elaborate game."

CHAPTER SIX

We arrived at the springs before dawn and my attendants set about occupying the mansion that had been built upon the grounds. The complex had been there since the last dynasty, a favorite retreat of many an emperor.

Yuan was situated in the chamber adjoining mine and I dismissed him to get some rest. The oil he had rubbed over me had seeped into my skin, imbuing it with the scent of flowers and reminding me of how I'd writhed in ecstasy while trapped beneath him. From now on, I would always be reminded of that when visiting my garden.

I left my robe on as I sank onto my bed, wanting the memory of Yuan's hands to linger a little longer. Next time, I vowed, his fingers would be replaced with something harder, bigger and ultimately more satisfying. He would penetrate me deeply while I lay pinned beneath him, and I would be powerless to do anything but take all of him as he thrust into me.

My lustful thoughts kept me from being able to fall asleep even though I had barely slept during the journey. As I tossed about on the bed, one that was much smaller than the bed in my palace, I wished that I had brought at least a few of my male concubines along, just to ease this restless tension.

Agitated, I went to the wall that separated Yuan's sleeping quarters from mine. There was a spyhole cut into the painting of a dragon and I raised myself onto my toes to look into the opening. Hazy morning light drifted in through the windows of the other chamber. After my eyes adjusted to the dimness, I saw Yuan sprawled onto the bed with all of his clothing removed. My heart skipped a beat and my throat went dry. I was being granted a gift.

His legs were parted. Between them, his organ stood as straight as a pillar, flushed and suffused with blood. His fist was closed around it, pumping hard up and down the shaft. The muscles of his forearm flexed and bulged and his head was thrown back, eyes closed. In his other hand, he held a length of golden silk to his nose.

I reached to feel around my shoulders. My shawl was missing.

Yuan had the material clutched to his face, inhaling deeply as he worked his fist in an increasing rhythm. My tongue cleaved to the roof of my mouth and my throat went painfully dry as I swallowed. Down below, the muscles of my sex squeezed tight.

Stubborn, impossible man. I wanted to fly through the doors and straddle him, sinking myself down onto every last inch of him. I would become the dream lover he was imagining in his head as he desperately inhaled my scent. *Mine.*

Why settle for five fingers when I was right here in the flesh?

But he was too far gone for that, even if he would have accepted. With a strangled sound, his hips jerked upward and pale fluid erupted from his organ, spilling over his knuckles. Gradually, his body relaxed into the bed. The gold shawl remained against his face as he slipped away into unknown dreams, finding the peaceful slumber that had eluded me.

For a thousand years now, as long as can be remembered, hot water naturally seeped up from the earth at this place. Originally, the water had collected in small mud holes, but over time the ponds had been dug out and widened until there were a series of connected pools, each of varying temperatures. An elegant garden with flowering trees and rock structures encompassed the bulk of the hot springs.

Yuan accompanied me to a bath house which sectioned off two of the bathing pools into a private oasis. A constant haze of vapor rose from the waters to envelop the chamber. The larger of the pools maintained the temperature of a comfortably warm steam bath for soaking, while the water from the smaller cleansing pool was just below scalding. Perfect for awakening and purifying the body.

I slipped off my robe and lowered myself into the hottest pool. The walls and bottom were lined with rock, and large, smooth stones were arranged beneath the water to serve as benches. I let my head fall back against the edge where wooden pillows had been placed as neck rests. The tension drained from my muscles as the steaming water surrounded me, flowing around me like an embrace.

The water level rose as Yuan entered the pool. His muscular leg brushed against mine as he settled into the water. I kept my eyes closed and my breathing even, reveling in the moment of quietness.

I had come here to get away from the imperial court and the treachery and danger that always gathered when men came together to vie for power. If only the hot springs could wash away the things I'd seen. The sight of my uncles huddled like animals inside iron cages. The look of sheer delight on my brother's face. As if it were all a game. A game...

When I opened my eyes, I found Yuan watching me, his gaze shuttered. He had his arms thrown back as he reclined against the stone edge. The position accentuated the muscles in his shoulders and he appeared at ease, as if offering himself to me. I knew it wasn't the case, but desire pooled hot and liquid in my belly. He had sought his release this morning, but I hadn't and it didn't take much to reawaken the dull throbbing of my sex.

It was much more enjoyable focusing on Yuan's inevitable surrender than the power struggles of the imperial court.

I smiled, remembering how he'd thrust into his fist while inhaling my scent. Immediately Yuan's heavy-lidded expression was replaced with a frown.

"It's only a matter of time, darling."

When he raised his eyebrow in question, I traced my toe

along his calf. He didn't pull away. Such a move would seem cowardly, of course. Instead, his lips twisted into a half-smile of his own. "It's been six days, Princess."

Such insolence! I'd watched him spill his seed over silken sheets only hours earlier.

"I have strong evidence that you're far from indifferent to me, Chu Yuan," I purred.

I rose from the pool, not caring to cover myself as water dripped from my skin onto the slate tile. I could feel his gaze on me as I sauntered to the main bath.

The water in this pool was cooler and the shock of it pierced into my skin like tiny pinpricks, further awakening my senses. I had the added pleasure of watching as Yuan rose to follow me. His manhood stood half-erect already and it was all I could do not to close my hands around the length of him the moment he lowered himself into the water beside me. The lips of my sex clenched around emptiness. It had been too long since I'd been properly filled. Properly fucked.

He had chosen to seat himself close, I noted. Yuan wasn't one to shrink away like a coward. That was one of the reasons I was so hungry for him.

"Is there something you can show me in four days that I haven't already seen?" he asked, his voice rougher than it had been only moments earlier. Could that possibly be anticipation I heard?

"Four days is plenty of time," I declared, though inwardly I was starting to despair. We had wasted so much time. "Perhaps I'll simply ask the Emperor to extend your services to me for a while longer."

His expression darkened at that, but mine was an empty threat. My attraction to Yuan had already awakened my brother's possessive nature. If I pleaded for any more than the ten days Ziye had given me, he would begin to think I'd become attached.

Had I become fixated? Yuan was a diversion who both challenged and amused me, but I was getting frustrated at his hardheadedness. I let none of that show as I glided through the water to him, my eyes narrowed coyly.

"Come now." I turned around and settled onto his lap, his front against my back. "Isn't this more enjoyable than long, boring days reviewing petitions and issuing decrees?"

His legs parted to allow me access and he lowered his hands beneath the water to grip my hips. Far from the denial I expected. His thick cock nestled into the cleft of my buttocks.

Seducing men, in my experience, had never required such plotting. I was a woman and willing. I was princess and in a position to offer power. But I didn't want to peddle influence to win Yuan over. I wanted him to burn for me the way I did for him.

With a sigh, I laid my head back against his shoulder. From there, I could look up at him. He regarded me with an expression that was certainly not as impassive as he intended. His eyes smoldered with heat.

"I know you think of it," I said breathlessly. "How perfectly our bodies will fit together."

I ground myself against him and he hardened further.

The smoke in his gaze turned to pure fire.

"By nature, all men and women's bodies complement one another," he replied stiffly.

With a sly look, I pushed my shoulders back and saw how his attention strayed toward my breasts as they lifted just above the surface of the water. The head of his organ teased against my opening, finding its rightful place of its own accord. I couldn't resist rounding my hips in a small circle, nudging him between my swollen lips.

The heated water was slippery with natural minerals. It would be so easy to push myself onto him and let him impale me. He would have me at his mercy, shuddering with ecstasy, with barely any effort on his part.

"You're shameless," he said in a low voice. There was no insult there, only a hint of awe.

"You like that I have no shame."

Yuan wasn't fighting. I could feel his thighs enclosing me like a vise and his breath came out in a shallow, broken rhythm.

I didn't want his passiveness, his mute acceptance. I wanted to feel him thrust into me so hard that I screamed with the pleasure of it. I wanted to squeeze him tight and spill his essence deep into my womb. Then there would be no doubt that we both wanted it.

But he was still resisting, even though I could feel his heart beating like a drum against my back.

"Perhaps my forward nature offends you," I suggested sweetly. "I can kneel at your feet. You can pretend I'm your concubine."

Groaning, he rested his forehead against mine, eyes forced shut. It made me want to devour him. I lowered my hips and the broad tip of his cock just entered me. The swollen flesh pulsed within my sensitive opening, making my knees go weak. *Now*, I urged him silently. *Please now.*

He dug his fingers into my hips, halting my movements, but doing nothing else to rebuke me. We were locked on a knife's edge of decision.

The entrance of one of my maidservants broke the impasse, at least for Yuan. He shifted away from me like an eel in water, leaving us once again side by side. I glared up at the girl, who was blushing too prettily and avoiding his gaze.

It agitated me to no end. Was she the sort of innocent, fresh-faced young thing he typically preferred?

"What is it?" I demanded.

"Chancellor Wu is here to see you."

At the mention of the high-ranking official's name, Yuan straightened even further.

"Well, it must be urgent. Bring him in."

Yuan's muscles coiled as if he were preparing to spring away, but there was no escape. Within moments, a middle-aged official dressed in an indigo robe arrived at the entrance. Wu was tall in stature and well-spoken by reputation. He was also known to despise me.

"Princess Shanyin." He bowed low, making all the prescribed gestures. His eyes fixed onto my face as if he couldn't see that I was soaking in the bathing pool naked or that Yuan was beside me, equally bared.

"What brings you here, Chancellor?"

"I am concerned for the wellbeing of the Emperor, most honorable Princess."

I snorted. "Then speak to the Emperor. You're a member of his inner court."

Wu had served in the court for over thirty years. He had witnessed the overthrow of my usurper uncle as well as the early death of my father. A man didn't survive such monumental power shifts without being uncommonly fortunate or clever.

"He has imprisoned the princes of Jian'an, Shanyang and Xiangdong in a matter unfitting for their stations," Wu continued.

My eyes glazed over at the mention of titles. "I know about my uncles. My brother is right to consider them potential enemies."

Wu bowed once more. "The princess is of course wise in her judgment."

Already I was tiring of this unwanted guest. "The Emperor will have his way with them and then let them go—or he won't. I have no say in his decisions."

"There is another incident the princess may not be aware of. Something troubling to myself as well as anyone concerned with the welfare of the empire. I'm certain the princess would want to be informed about it."

Wu couldn't keep from sounding condescending when he spoke to me.

"What is it?" I asked, irritated.

"At the same time his uncles were imprisoned, the

Emperor had their wives and daughters brought from their homes and installed within the palace."

A sick feeling snaked through me. "And why is this of any interest to me?"

"You know what your Emperor-brother is capable of. Have you not any sympathy for these women and children?"

"And you wish for me to intervene on their behalf," I remarked coldly. My chest had squeezed so tight I could barely breathe.

"You were born a woman, Princess. I beg of you to use your influence over the Emperor to guide him the ways of justice and mercy."

"Of course. We women are all kind and soft, full of justice and mercy." My tone was soft, then sharp. "Did you not tell the Emperor that I was a corrupting influence? Did you not urge the other ministers of the court to petition for my removal from the imperial palace?"

Wu bowed deeply. "That was long before this servant became aware of the princess's virtuous nature. I beg of you, in these circumstances, we must be willing to look past such disagreements. For the sake of the empire."

Willing? Even now, the chancellor's attitude remained disdainful and superior. He wanted my assistance despite looking down at me as if I were no more than dust beneath his heel. He wanted to put this burden on my shoulders.

"You appeal to my womanly mercy," I replied with a sneer. "Where were all these princesses—my aunts and cousins—while I was being held captive? And who had the audacity to call me virtuous? As you can see, I'm no more virtuous than you are."

Keeping my eyes fixed on Wu's face, I reached between Yuan's legs to take hold of his manhood. It had reduced in length and size, but still remained firm to the touch. Yuan jerked as my hand closed over him. Slowly, I stroked the length of Yuan's impressive manhood beneath the water, taking my time while I smiled at the chancellor, challenging him to spout more of his drivel at me. Wu finally glanced away, embarrassed.

"I'll consider your request," I said, full of enough insolence to match Wu's disdain.

The chancellor nodded and ducked away. The moment he was gone, Yuan shoved me away from him and rose from the pool, not caring that he gave me a full view of his naked physique.

"Are there no limits to your immorality?" he growled.

"Immoral?" I snapped back. Normally, it would have amused me to taunt and ignore the insults, but with Yuan my every nerve ending was pulsing and raw. "Men like Chancellor Wu have blood on their hands from a lifetime of treachery and intrigue, yet I'm immoral for taking men to my bed?"

Yuan stared at me, his eyes cold and jaw hard. Despite the warmth of the bathing pool, a chill ran down my spine.

"I am not your slave. Never use me like that again or you will regret it," he warned, storming from the chamber without bothering to don his robe.

My personal chamber was empty when I returned to it, but I didn't question where my attendants had gone. My hair was still damp and I had nothing covering me but a sheer layer of silk. There were too many things on my mind. Despite what I'd told the chancellor, I was thinking of my aunts and cousins. More importantly, I was thinking of Ziye. Killing his enemies was one thing, but their wives and children? Even I wasn't that much of a monster.

I searched through the desk in the corner, producing a writing box from one of the drawers. A message sent by fast horse would reach the palace long before my caravan, but what was I to say to the Emperor to penetrate the black shell of his madness?

My dearest brother, I would write. Do not make any grand gestures until your trusted sister is once more by your side, when I can share in both your sorrows and triumphs.

I lifted the lid from the lacquered case to reveal the calligraphy brushes and inkstone nestled inside. As I reached for a brush, strong arms took hold of me. The contents of the case scattered over the floor as I was thrown down and my legs pinned by an immoveable weight.

I fought. Or I tried to fight. The wind had been knocked out of me by the impact and I gasped, unable to find breath. A man straddled my hips, holding my wrists in an iron grip. For a moment I didn't recognize him, and his features took on the twisted visages of my nightmares, one face blending into another and then another above me while I was held down.

"No one will come for you, Princess. I told them you didn't want to be disturbed."

The hold on my wrists loosened momentarily, but not long enough for me to break free. He held both of them just as easily with one large hand as he did with two. With his free hand, he tugged the sash from around my waist.

My heart beat frantically and my throat clenched with fear, but the voice cut through the nightmare darkness. It was familiar. The shape of him above me and even his touch, as rough as it was, wasn't completely foreign. And the smell of his skin...

"Yuan?" I choked out.

I blinked through the momentary haze and saw it was indeed him, but his expression was one I'd never seen before. His eyes were dark and his teeth bared. He was seething with anger and utterly, completely focused on his task.

The length of silk looped around my wrists; once, twice, before Yuan knotted it tight. I tried to struggle once more when he secured the other end to the foot of the desk, stretching my arms over my head. The heavy rosewood refused to move when I tugged against it. Yuan merely looked down at me, watching with cruel interest as I writhed and fought to no avail.

He was naked still, not having bothered to clothe himself after leaving the bath house. I was also barely dressed, my thin covering falling open in the skirmish. His organ pressed against my sex as he straddled me and it jerked luridly when I twisted my hips to try and unseat him.

"You can even shout for them and they wouldn't come to your aid," he said, his tone cold. "Because your servants believe I am your little plaything and the louder you scream, the more you are enjoying all the things you are having me do to you."

Despite his words, he produced another length of cloth—my gossamer shawl he'd used while pleasuring himself—and gagged me with it. The material cut into the corners of my mouth, muffling my words.

"But I think I like having you like this more," he finished.

I was completely helpless beneath him, unable to move, to taunt or tease or command. Was this how it would happen? I had wanted him to take me, but not in anger. Not forced against my will.

Yuan lowered his hands to my breasts while I could do nothing but watch, sobbing in protest. I jumped at his first touch, but as he cupped the soft weights in his palms, I was stricken by the same sense I had of him the first time he'd undressed me. He could have been rough with me. Or cold and impersonal—everything else about his demeanor spoke of his intention to treat me like I'd treated him. But there was both a sense of care and mastery in his touch.

My heart thudded against my ribs and I knew he could sense it as he kneaded my flesh, testing the feel of me in his hands. His thumbs passed lightly over my nipples, both of them at once. Pleasure, pure and raw, raced through me.

My heart beat even harder, but with more anticipation than fear.

I had no idea what he intended to do with me, but I knew he was still enraged by how I'd flaunted him in front of the chancellor. I stared into his face to search for some answer, but there was none as his endlessly black eyes fixed onto me. He merely repeated the slow caress of his thumbs over my nipples, forcing them into painfully hard points as he watched me; face blank, but eyes blazing hot.

"This is what you wanted, isn't it, Princess?" he asked in a dangerous tone.

I shook my head, the gag preventing me from anything more than a mewl of protest. It pleased him, my resistance. His cock was now hard and hot between my thighs and my head swam with confusion. Should I resist or not? And if I did resist him, would it only provoke him more?

And was that exactly what I wanted to do?

His lips lifted grimly when I shifted my hips away from his member. But he didn't thrust himself into me. That would have been too easy, the demon. Instead he reached for one of the brushes lying on the floor and held it up so I could see it.

It was finely made, with a long elegant stalk fashioned of bamboo. The head was made from rabbit hair and shaped to a point for delicate precision.

"You commanded me to touch you, did you not?"

Yuan swiped the brush over my cheek, then down the bridge of my nose. Squirming, I tried to duck away. It tickled.

After a pause, he touched the brush to my lips which were distended beneath the gag. This caress was completely unexpected, making my chest squeeze tight. The look in his eyes was both wicked and playful, but it shifted darkly as the instrument feathered down over my throat and collarbone. Watching my face intently, Yuan brought the tip down over my left nipple, drawing a slow circle over the pebbled flesh.

I closed my eyes as my back rose off the floor. Yuan was relentless, circling, then teasing in a never-ending pattern. As I squirmed and writhed, my sex flooded to demand more. When I thought I could take it no longer, he moved the brush tip over to my other breast. I cried out against the gag as Yuan tormented me, circling and stroking while I shook my head violently from side to side, trying to thrash free but failing.

The delicate stroke of the brush was tantalizing at first, each caress of the tip over my breast echoing down below in my sex. But the arousal quickly became overwhelming until every inch of me was on fire and I wanted to scream.

I did scream. "Stop!" I shouted against the gag, but it only came out as a muffled grunt. "Stop, stop…"

Each word was both a plea and a moan. I sobbed with relief as the brush moved away to feather over the underside of my breasts, then to my stomach. My skin tingled all over and I flinched whenever the brush found a particularly sensitive spot.

My relief was short-lived. The brush continued in slow strokes down an inevitable path over my hips and then lower still. He wouldn't dare—

Yuan had my lower body pinned while he straddled above me. He shifted now and took hold of one of my legs as I tried to kick at him. With a hand set at the crook of my knee, he held my leg against his side, bent at an angle which naturally opened me to him.

"Why fight me now, Shanyin? You've made your desires clear from the start."

The brush moved over my mound, lingering to prolong my torture. The moment stretched out into eternity and I could hear the sound of my ragged breathing. The thunder of my pulse filled my ears.

I did fight him. I fought him hard. The thought of what he was going to do to me was unbearable. There was nothing I could do to stop it.

The very tip of the brush slid over the pearl of my sex and I jumped, but Yuan used his weight and strength to anchor me to the ground. His gaze bore into me.

The sensation was delicate, almost elusive, yet I could feel it everywhere. My nipples, already worked to a point beyond pleasure, throbbed endlessly. My chest squeezed tight. Down below, my inner muscles clenched and pulsed, unfulfilled.

He leaned in closer, widening my legs as he positioned his shoulders between them. I felt his fingers on my outer lips, parting them wetly with a soft, slick sound. The brush head stroked over my slit, dipping into the well of moisture gathering there. Then it lifted to stroke directly over the hard bud of my sex.

It was as awful and as incredible as I'd feared. He repeated the movement, soft bristles dipping into my slit and then flicking over the small nub. I thrashed against my bonds and bit hard against the gag, making incoherent sounds like a wild animal. My knees fell open of their own accord now; mindless, blind with pleasure.

Please. Please, I moaned against the gag. The tip of the brush became soaked with my fluids, making each stroke sharper, the sensation more acute. But the fine rabbit hair was too delicate to deliver me. Even when I strained my hips upward, begging silently, the pressure wasn't enough to give me the release I so desperately wanted. *Needed.*

And through it all, Yuan lorded over me, watching my descent into madness. I didn't care. I was at his mercy. I would do, would *become* whatever he wanted. His whore. His slave. If he would just let me come.

The motion of the brush stopped and I sobbed out loud, tears flooding my eyes. I had never been so aroused. Brought to the edge only to be denied.

"What was it you threatened?" Yuan asked. His voice was thick, saturated with desire. His cock lay heavy against his thighs. "You said you would cut my tongue out?"

He bent his head and granted me the soft, wet stroke of his tongue over my aching sex. I sobbed once more, but this time in gratitude.

"This tongue?" he taunted, his breath hot against my sex before he worked me with his lips and mouth.

My hips strained upward. My legs trembled and I tried to close them around Yuan to clamp him to me. If he stopped now, I would die. But he didn't. Thank heaven above and earth below. He flicked his tongue in small circles, lighter as my flesh became more sensitive. My cries blended together into one endless moan as he took me higher, easing me with the flat of his tongue when it became too much, then using the tip with unerring precision.

The orgasm shattered through me and I was gasping, crying, undone. I thought wildly that it would finally happen now. Yuan had demonstrated his dominance over me and now he would take his own pleasure.

Instead he pinned my hips down with his hands as the last of my shudders began to subside. He continued to lick at my flesh, but the touch became gentle, loving. Even so, it was too much. I tried to close my legs, turning my hips away and curling my knees toward me. Yuan wouldn't allow it. His hands exerted more force as needed, just enough to keep me trapped.

Soon the soft strokes became harder, deliberate. He worked me once more toward climax and I tried to shake my head no, but I went unheeded. I could see the top of his head dipping low as he pulled me closer, his hands sliding beneath me to grasp my buttocks and lift my sex to him. He dipped his tongue just inside my folds and then pushed deeper, spearing into me.

I came again. I had no choice.

Afterward, my muscles went slack and I lay in a pool on the floor, drained and exhausted. I tried to close my eyes, but Yuan wasn't done.

"But this isn't what you really want, is it Shanyin?"

My eyes flew open at the hardness of his tone. The two orgasms had left me sated, sapped of all will, but Yuan hadn't yet found release.

He slid up my side, dark intent in every movement. I became alert once more, my pulse racing. He stopped once he was crouched beside my head and reached down to untie the gag around my mouth before taking hold of the base of his manhood with one hand. His shaft lifted in anticipation.

"This is what you want." He leaned down and his voice was a rumble in my ear. "You want this cock deep in your cunt."

The stark words sent a dark shiver through me. My mouth was still sore from the gag and I ran my tongue over my lips and swallowed. Yuan watched every movement with interest. His other hand curved around the back of my head, his touch almost gentle.

"If you want me inside you, then get me hard, Princess. Suck me so I can fuck you."

I'd never heard that growl in his voice before. Or the language of the gutter from his lips. He was already hard, but he pressed his organ against my lips regardless; not roughly, but insistent. The hand at the nape of my neck tilted me toward him and my lips parted of their own accord. He slid his length inside my mouth, forcing my lips wide. I was rendered hot and helpless at the feel of him filling my mouth until he was all I could taste and smell.

I moaned around his thick member and Yuan stiffened,

his eyelids growing heavy. I could feel the shudder that ran through him against the walls of my mouth.

"Suck me hard," he urged.

Tied up as I was, there was little I could do but close my lips around him and draw him deeper into my mouth. I had taken men this way before, both larger and smaller than Yuan. Each one was different, but in some ways the same. I worked my tongue against the underside of his cock where I knew men to be particularly sensitive. Yuan's organ twitched, hitting against my teeth as he grew impossibly thicker.

Up until then he'd been patient, not moving while I became accustomed to him. But that moment was brief. Yuan's hand tightened in my hair and with a small pull of his hips, he withdrew. I breathed shallowly around the space created before he pushed back in, pausing to readjust the hand at my head. Then he pulled back and thrust again, in and out in a slow rhythm.

At first I licked my tongue over the head of his cock whenever he withdrew, but soon it was impossible. His thrusts became faster, harder as his breathing quickened. Though he was on his knees, I was the supplicant. My mouth, my body was nothing but an instrument for him to use.

I moaned around him as he pushed deeper, both in pleasure and protest. His hips continued thrusting as he grasped my head with both hands now, one cradled against my cheek, the other still at the nape of my neck to hold me exactly where he wanted me while he took his pleasure.

The head of his cock butted against my throat and I flinched, gagging. Yuan didn't stop, but he seemed to thrust more carefully even as the rhythm increased.

By now, my jaw was aching and my neck stiff from being held at an odd angle. I knew he had no intention of fucking me now—if he'd ever intended it in the first place. He was too far gone for that. His entire body tensed, every muscle rigid. His face was fixed in a mask of agony and ecstasy.

He shifted closer, repositioning his knees so he could thrust into my mouth in shorter and faster strokes. It was difficult to breathe, but I knew it wouldn't be much longer. I willed his release to happen soon. Every moment of his pleasure now was traded for my pain, but I gave it willingly.

Suddenly his muscles locked and he went utterly still except for the pulse of his cock as he released his fluids into me. He tasted of salt and bitter tea as I swallowed. I could feel his hands shaking on either side of my face as he spent the last of his essence down my throat.

Then he let go of me abruptly and withdrew his organ from my mouth, still half-erect but softening quickly. He turned away and sat on the floor, knees raised and head lowered as if in meditation. His chest heaved as he fought to catch his breath.

I licked my lips, catching a trace of the salty-bitter taste of him as I waited for Yuan to find his voice. It didn't happen. Several long minutes later, he was still turned away from me, shoulders bent.

"Yuan, untie me," I said firmly.

When I repeated the order, his head whipped around. His eyes flashed with anger. "Maybe I should keep you there and torment you for the rest of the day," he snapped. "At my mercy now."

It wasn't too long ago when our situation had been reversed, with him tied to my bed. But here was the difference between us. Yuan had taken control. He'd given pleasure and taken it while I was helpless and writhing beneath him, yet he was the one broken.

My hands were still bound over my head and my mouth sore from being used. Between my legs, I could feel the wetness where his tongue and my juices had mingled.

"Untie me now," I commanded in a tone that said I was Princess Shanyin and mere men did not deny me. "It will take us all day to return to the imperial palace and I need to go to the Emperor as soon as possible. Before it's too late."

CHAPTER SEVEN

Yuan rode outside the litter on the journey back to the imperial palace and I didn't protest. Instead I slept.

My dreams. What did I dream about in the aftermath of being tied up and tormented to multiple orgasms? One would think it would be wild orgies and beautiful naked men, lining up to take their turn with me.

It was nothing like that.

As the transport rocked me with its swaying motion, I dreamed about flowers. The flowers in my garden which always looked so pure despite growing from dirt and decay. I ran my fingers across the cool petals and touched the tips of the green leaves.

One bloom in the center looked withered, but I merely plucked it and tossed it aside so it wouldn't mar the beauty of the rest of the garden. But then I found another so I plucked it as well. Soon everywhere I looked, every plant was black and shriveled, eaten through with worms. Dying.

Soon, I was no longer searching for wilted ones to remove, but for a single fresh flower. There had to be one left and I had to find it.

I woke up still searching and wishing I'd dreamt about orgies. Or at least about Yuan finally giving into his desires, though he was starting to confound me as much as the dream. I opened the curtain and peered outside to see the sun dipping below the horizon. Yuan sat tall astride his horse, set against the orange sky.

I didn't call out to him and he very pointedly did not turn to look at me. The sight of his silhouette was enough to make my insides flutter.

Was Yuan still angry with me? I remembered how he'd bound my wrists, rendering me helpless. Perhaps I wanted him to be angry. Men who had no control over their emotions were easily blinded by rage. Those men became unpredictable and violent. They were monsters to be feared, but for a man like Yuan, anger aroused all sorts of passions.

He was slipping through my fingers like water. Selfishly, I wanted him to feel something for me when he was gone. Anger had a way of worming its way deep into one's heart and lodging there. At least anger wasn't indifference.

Whether or not Yuan succumbed to my demands, I only had four days left.

Our arrival at the imperial palace was met without circumstance. Evening was upon us and the guardsmen managed a cursory inspection before allowing the caravan inside. I immediately sent a message to my brother by runner to announce that I had returned.

I held the curtain of the litter open while I gave the command and I saw Yuan regarding me with a dark stare. The memory of his hands clamped around my head assailed me. I could almost taste him on my tongue. I let the curtain fall back in place while my heart continued to pound.

The moment already felt a lifetime away. While Yuan and the rest of the entourage returned to my palatial estate, I alone went to see the Emperor.

I entered the gates of my brother's inner sanctum and was met by the warm glow of red lanterns swinging from the eaves. A soft, haunting melody floated through the empty garden, presenting a tranquil scene that was at odds with the lawlessness and debauchery Chancellor Wu had warned me of. Perhaps my brother had found some peace while I was away. I could only pray it was so.

A hulking ox of a man blocked the doors to the bedchamber. My brother Ziye chose to surround himself with fearsome bodyguards of whom Bataar was likely the most menacing, at least by appearance.

As the story was told, Bataar had survived a wolf attack as a youth and the animal had taken half his face before he killed it. The ragged scars were still visible with one cruel gash cutting directly over his left eye which had been blinded in the attack. It was useless, covered by a milky film.

The brutish guard bowed gracelessly at my approach. He kept his head lowered as I approached, as was proper, but I could still see his face as he was so much taller than I. It was a difficult face to look at, as ruined as it was.

I wondered why Ziye chose to keep him in such a prominent place when it was tradition for the Emperor to choose the most attractive of attendants. I suppose he did it to ward away any would-be assassins. I myself had selected my concubines and maidservants for their physical beauty. Why surround myself with any reminders of the ugliness of the world?

Without slowing my stride, I aimed for the door. Bataar stood aside, but appeared to hesitate as if he wanted to address me. That would have been highly unusual—there was little reason for so lowly a servant to speak to a princess.

The moment passed and the guardsman pushed the door open for me. I entered the sitting room to find two ladies, one older and one young, playing a duet involving a stringed pipa and bamboo flute. Ziye was nowhere in sight, though he was expecting me.

The musicians continued uninterrupted and their song shifted to a sentimental, almost melancholy mood. I waved them into silence just as a figure stepped through the curtain that separated the sitting room from the bedchamber.

I halted to stare. The woman was a handful of years older than me, though still youthful in appearance. The pins in her hair had come loose and her robe was in disarray. The vermillion tint on her lips had been smeared, but she made no effort to clean it.

As she reached me, the woman paused and I saw recognition flicker in her eyes before she ducked her head and hurried from the room. Ziye came out a moment later, sauntering through the curtain with a self-indulgent smile.

His robe was open in front and his trousers haphazardly tied.

"Elder Sister," he greeted. "Did you enjoy your tryst at the hot springs with your new lover?"

I pressed my lips tight, refusing to be deterred. "That was Liu Shang's wife."

His grin widened. "Ah, but I'm learning the benefits of an older, more experienced woman. She sucks me like a goddess. I almost wanted to fall on my knees afterward, to thank her."

My frown deepened. "She's our aunt."

Ziye made a face and pointedly turned his shoulder to me as he stared at the musicians. The women kept their head bowed and eyes averted, though I caught a few nervous glances exchanged between them. My brother remained silent, appearing to weigh some decision for a long time before shooing them away.

"No man will tolerate another man claiming what's his," I scolded when we were alone. "You'll make a bitter enemy of our uncle."

"Liu Shang has no say in this matter!" my brother retorted. "He's still locked up in a cage, like a pig awaiting slaughter."

He made pig-like noises in his throat which would have seemed childish were I not completely chilled by his demeanor. He was becoming more aggressive and moodier by the day.

"And besides, I'm not another man. Am I not the Son of Heaven, powerful and god-like?"

Instead of seating himself on the benches and pillows in the room, Ziye went instead to the raised dais where his throne stood. There was one in every room where the Emperor might choose to have an audience. He sprawled onto it, one leg raised insolently.

"And when did you become so uptight, sister? You never answered me about Lord Chu Yuan. Does my latest gift please you? Are you so satisfied that you've forsaken all your other lovers for him alone?"

I didn't like the sharp edge to his words. I would not play this game, the one where he blamed me for his degeneration. With a deep breath, I went to stand at the foot of the dais.

"I know our uncles are our enemies and our greatest threat," I began soothingly. "But they have armies and factions behind them. Outwardly, we must keep the peace."

My counsel sounded hollow in my own ears. What did I know of politics? My arguments were thinner than paper, but Ziye's shoulders sank and some of the edgy restlessness drained from him.

"I hate them," he said, appearing lost and exhausted. "They still try to pull strings in court, forcing my hand."

"Then we won't let them," I assured.

I convinced him to release our uncles, but to send them into exile. I urged him to release their wives and families as well, keeping only one heir from each household in the palace as hostage, just as our uncles had done to us. Over the next hours, I wrote out the decrees myself and put them in front of my brother to sign and stamp with the imperial seal.

Ziye's hand paused over the decree that would release Liu Shang and his wife. It had to be the excitement of besting an enemy that had him so fixated with the woman. He had enjoyed her favors for only a day and, though far from elderly, she was past her spring years.

Firmly, I tapped the space at the bottom of the scroll and my brother affixed his seal.

This is how one goes about wresting power, I realized with a heavy sense of dread as I watched the jade chop press down on the document to leave its red imprint.

The thought was ridiculous. There was no way I could act as regent for Ziye. I was a woman and only seven years older than my brother, without any knowledge of how to rule. When our father had taken over the throne, my only thought was to drown in excess and pleasure to make up for all the years of living in fear.

After the decrees were complete, I sent for retainers to have them carried out immediately. Then I had a sleeping elixir of mimosa bark steeped in green tea brought in for Ziye and put him to bed.

"Will you leave me now?" he asked as the herbal brew made his eyelids heavy.

"Once you're asleep, Imperial Majesty."

"No, Sister." His eyes flashed fiercely. "Will you leave me for Chu Yuan?"

I laughed. "Hardly."

"You're obsessed with him," my brother insisted stubbornly. "I've seen you."

My stomach turned on the last part. I didn't dare ask him what he meant. "Do you think any one man could enchant your sister?"

"I can smell him on you," he accused, his tone more hurt than angry.

"That's absurd."

"You're going to ask to be wed to him. You'll belong to him and not me."

His jaw clenched and the look of hatred in his eyes made my blood run cold. Ziye was fighting the elixir to stay awake and I willed for him to go to sleep.

I stroked his hair back from his face, something I had not done for a long time. Despite the affectionate gesture, my chest felt as if stones had been placed upon it to slowly crush the air from my lungs. I looked into his eyes, searching for the boy I once knew, but found no trace of him. For the first time, I was as frightened of Ziye as I was frightened for him.

"Didn't we always say our fates were linked, you and I?" I asked gently.

Finally Ziye nodded drowsily and let his eyes fall closed. "You and I," he echoed, the last part trailing off. "I trust no one but you, Shanyin."

Like everyone else, I had learned exactly what needed to be said to please the Emperor. In doing so, I'd become just like all the other cronies and sycophants, kowtowing for his favor.

I remained there, staring at him while he slept. They say that in sleep all men look innocent and vulnerable. My brother did look young once more, with the harsh sneer wiped from his face. But I couldn't see past what he'd become in the year since he'd taken the throne.

He was a tyrant. A hateful, vengeful creature who struck out like a storm, with no consideration for what it destroyed. But as far as I could see, he was no worse than any emperor who had come before him, including our father.

When I left the imperial quarters, the bodyguard Bataar was still standing like a guardian lion at the entrance.

"Princess Shanyin," he called after me, his tone rough around the honorific.

I turned. "Yes?" I asked, perhaps a bit brusquely. It was late. Very late.

"Has—has the princess been to the Bamboo Hall?" he asked haltingly.

His hesitant manner was a contrast to his frightening appearance. While he averted his one good eye, the blind one seemed to stare directly at me. I had to bid him to speak before he would continue.

"There's blood everywhere," he told me. "Blood was shed there this very day."

Yuan's room was dark when I slipped inside, carrying a small oil lamp with me to light my way. The windows were open and the night air was just starting to cool. He wore a pale under-tunic and trousers to bed and lay on his back without any covers. Blankets were unnecessary during the summer months.

I placed the oil lamp on a side table and left it burning as I climbed into bed beside him. His hair had been let down from its topknot and fell about his face. In the eerie flicker of the light he appeared even more beautiful and more unattainable.

"Yuan," I murmured softly.

"Princess," he responded.

"Were you asleep?"

"No," he admitted and I was glad. I wanted him to lie awake thinking of me as I did of him.

I curled myself against his side, fitting my curves to the hard, solid frame of his body. Tension traveled through him as I did so.

"You have thirty lovers in your harem at your service." Yuan kept his eyes closed and I could see him swallowing as he spoke.

So this is the game he wanted to play; me the sex-starved fox demon and he the steadfast, righteous hero. Even though he'd had his tongue thrust inside me just this morning. The thought made my sex clench.

"Thirty-one," I corrected.

But not for much longer. I could feel a sharp pang in my chest as it constricted around my heart.

I ran the flat of my palm over his chest, finding where the beat of his heart was strongest and resting there. I had to stretch over him to reach his throat. With my chest against his shoulder, I kissed the side of his neck gently like a rain of flowers. Then I scraped my teeth lightly over the sensitive skin, reveling in the small shudder that ran through him.

"Imagine I'm your long lost love, if you have to," I whispered against his ear before taking the lobe between my teeth.

His hands came up to settle around my waist, but he didn't push me away. I reached down to undo his undergarments and push them aside as much as I could before mounting him. I was still clothed. Selfishly, I wanted him to undress me. There was something about undressing myself during sex that felt too much like I was doing a servant's task.

I felt his cock hardening beneath my pelvic bone before he spoke. "She's no longer alive."

I stilled while straddled above him. An odd sensation curled tight in my stomach. I didn't know if I was more bothered by him revealing such a personal detail to me or by his admission that he did indeed have a long lost love.

"Does this remind you of her too much?" I ran my hands along his arms, an innocent enough touch, but a sensual enough one to make my meaning clear. Was this truly why he refused to give in to his desires?

"We never kissed or touched. We rarely even spoke."

"Oh. You were arranged to be married, then."

"Last spring, but it was not meant to be."

I didn't push further, surprised that Yuan had revealed something so personal to me at all. It was more intimate, more invasive than having his cock thrusting into my mouth.

Bracing my palms, I lowered myself so I could lie over him. I liked the warm feel of him pressed to me from neck to toe.

"Do you think of her to help you resist me?" I asked shamelessly.

It was a tactless and deplorable question to ask, but I was the immoral Princess Shanyin. I was also one woman jealous of another, even if her rival was only a ghost. Heartache had the potential of lasting a lifetime, even into the next life.

"I wouldn't dishonor her memory by bringing her into your bed," he replied bluntly.

I should have been insulted, but I was already too numb by all that I had seen and learned that night to be wounded. Bataar had taken me to the Bamboo Hall, where my brother regularly cavorted with his palace women, to show me the bloodstains on the floor. He described how my brother had brought in a row of princesses, our aunts and their daughters, and ordered them to lie down on the floor so his attendants could have their way with them. When one of our aunts refused, Ziye had the woman's children dragged in and publicly executed before the gathering. She was then beheaded right there in the hall.

I sank against Yuan, my head resting on his shoulder. He was warm and undemanding, but it wasn't enough. I needed something to chase away the demons. The thought of summoning my harem to satisfy me left me cold.

"I don't want to sleep alone tonight," I confessed and immediately regretted it.

I sounded weak. Sentimental. Princess Shanyin took what she wanted.

Once again I laid my hand on his chest. I explored the expanse of his torso and the plane of his abdomen, my hands roaming at leisure. I dipped lower to round over the curve of his hip.

"Does this tempt you?" I asked quietly, as a matter-of-fact.

There was a long pause before he answered, his voice deep with a rasp of desire. "You know it does."

"But you'll fight it."

"Yes."

I knew he would and he'd likely succeed, but I didn't care. "Then fight it."

I explored his naked body with my hands and mouth, taking my time. Not an inch of him was neglected except for that selfish cock of his which twitched hungrily as I ran my hands over the strong muscles of his legs. I planted a kiss high on his inner thigh to make his breath catch, purposely letting my hair fall to tease over him. But I left his organ untouched.

Let him keep that part to himself. Tonight I wanted everything else.

I needed this more than I needed him embedded inside me right now. Sex by its nature was a crash of lightning and thunder that shook the foundations of the world before quickly dissipating. He'd spill over the sheets and be done, slumbering away, while I would be left awake and alone.

Instead I awakened every part of him and claimed it for

myself. Yuan shuddered as I sucked his toes into my mouth and I was filled with pure, wicked pleasure. I turned him over to explore his backside and he was a willing puppet in my hands.

His shoulders were a joy to behold. I imagined what pursuits he engaged in to keep them so strong. Archery, most likely. A favored pastime of the aristocracy. Or perhaps wrestling, his body naked and oiled. I straddled him and dug my thumbs into the hard muscle, feeling his body relax and sigh. I could be kind as well as cruel. Didn't he know that?

I climbed off him and my hands followed the curve of his spine to his buttocks. I gave the hard globes a squeeze before raking my nails lightly over them. He groaned and his hips jerked against the bed.

But I was here for my pleasure and not his. I wanted to tease him to the point of pain, but do nothing to release his suffering. By the time I turned him onto his back, his hands were clenched around air and his breathing ragged.

I snuggled once more into the crook of his arm and took hold of his hand. It felt heavy in mine as I brought him between my legs.

"I'm here," I told him, directing his hand into the dewy wetness of my slit.

His eyes were squeezed shut. His expression was one of agony and his member was engorged with blood, stabbing straight into the air. Let him revel in his bitter triumph.

I couldn't resist circling his finger over my aching bud, slippery with my juices. His hands were so much rougher than mine, providing the perfect pressure over the slick, soft flesh. A delicious shiver ran down my spine.

"Come find me," I whispered, leaving his hand drenched in my sex before curling against him to fall asleep.

CHAPTER EIGHT

I half expected to wake up with Yuan moving deep inside me, unable to restrain himself. Instead it was the morning sunlight that woke me. Yuan was turned away on his side. My only consolation was that his hands were curled into tight fists, telling me that at least his sleep wasn't a peaceful one.

Irritated, I rose from the bed to return to my chamber. As I walked, I could feel my sex still swollen and unfulfilled from the night before. Why was I being so indulgent of him? Teasing him, even gratifying him with my hands and mouth, which only rewarded him for resisting. I turned to look over my shoulder at him once more before straightening.

The worst of it was that I had shown Yuan how weak I could be. How much I yearned for the attentions of someone who wasn't a servant or a slave. Someone I didn't completely command.

He continued to lord that over me and I was done with it.

I summoned Tai and Jiyi. It had been six days since I'd requested anyone from my harem and they were eager to see me. The moment Tai came to the bedchamber, he

124

caught me up in his arms and kissed me, not waiting for my command. He held me eagerly against him while his mouth moved hungrily over mine. Normally I would have frowned upon such a display of possessiveness, but it was hard to fault such open enthusiasm.

"Don't be greedy! The princess summoned both of us, you ox."

Jiyi's taunt was delivered with his typical good-natured charm and I smiled as he swept me into his embrace. He was leaner in build than Tai. His features were also more fine-boned while Tai was roughly cut, but they complimented each other perfectly. My eye never tired of looking at the two of them. There were so many differences and nuances to appreciate.

I had always thought the two of them combined would be the ultimate lover. Now I didn't know if such a man existed any more.

"We missed you, Princess." Jiyi nibbled my neck flirtatiously. I confess, it felt wonderful to touch and be touched so freely. "We were afraid you were still angry at us for that incident on the polo field."

"I *am* still angry at you." I affected a cross look while lifting his chin with the tip of my finger. "Your princess could have been trampled to death."

"I can't bear to think of it! We would have been entombed with you," Jiyi insisted.

I slipped from his embrace to sit back onto the bed, glancing from Tai to Jiyi. "Come here and regain my good favor, then," I said with a look that was full of smoke and fire.

Jiyi's clothes were already half off when he tackled me. I fell onto my back, giggling. Tai was more deliberate in his movements. He stood at the edge of the bed, presenting a lovely spectacle for my pleasure as he disrobed. All the while, Jiyi had his arms around me, deftly peeling my own robe from my shoulders.

"We took it upon ourselves to punish Feng for what happened on the field," Tai reported, quite serious. He stripped away his trousers last to reveal his already hardening member, which jutted upward proudly.

There was a reason they were my favorites. Tai and Jiyi were capable of being teasing, bawdy, wicked. Shifting to whatever suited my mood so that I rarely tired of them.

Tai was certainly the most striking of my concubines. They were all selected for their beauty, but he was a natural leader among them. I had seen it from the start. He had tried at times to take command of me as well, but that was when I'd put him in his place. We had an understanding, but at times like these, when he looked at me with such fierce hunger in his eyes, I knew he would always push at those boundaries. My heart pounded as I waited for him to approach. I loved the element of danger he provided, though I knew in the end he was completely mine.

Jiyi was different. He was honey-tongued in every way, able to gauge my moods and soothe away dark thoughts with clever words and good humor. His hands were equally skilled at discovering the hidden and secret nuances of my body. He could send me to heaven within minutes with his mouth, licking and sucking until I begged for more. Then he'd hold me afterwards and shower me with pretty words, making me smile, making me laugh.

I'd missed them, I admitted defiantly. For the last week I'd allowed myself to become fixated on one man, giving him all my attention. I knew that was a seed for disaster.

Jiyi unlaced my bodice and removed it, leaving me completely naked. Then he moved behind me to cup both my breasts in his hands. Not willing to be left out, Tai climbed onto the bed as well, closing his large hands around my ankles; another possessive gesture.

I shot him a look and Tai immediately loosened his grip. I was not in the mood to be tested this morning. The insolent aristocrat sleeping in the next chamber had tested my patience all week and I was spent.

"He's been pining for you," Jiyi confided, fondling my breasts in a way that had me melting back against him. He tossed Tai a sly look and then bent to speak low in my ear. "He kept on calling out your name while climaxing. I would have scolded him, were my mouth not occupied."

I laughed and Jiyi joined his deeper voice with mine, gathering me close as we shared in the jest. Even the fire in Tai's expression tempered, becoming warm as he stroked his hands up my legs to bring him closer to both of us. They were my chosen concubines, my slaves, but I cared for them. I believed they cared for me as well. Perhaps it was merely a pretty fantasy, but what was all of life if not a dream?

Perhaps it was the laughter that roused Yuan from his

bed. He appeared through the curtain a moment later, still dressed in his sleeping clothes, to see me completely naked in the embrace of two men.

Something curled tight within me at the sight of him. His eyes locked onto mine and my heart hammered within my chest. What was this hold he had over me?

The smile faded from my lips and Tai detected the change in me. He looked over his shoulder and immediately his spine straightened. He shifted positions to rearrange himself by my side as he faced off against Yuan.

"Princess Shanyin," Yuan greeted me as if the other two weren't there.

Lazily, Tai draped an arm over my knee and ran his fingers lightly along the inside of my thigh, stopping just shy of my sex. All the while he kept his gaze on his rival. I permitted the small power play and was glad I did when I saw how Yuan's pupils darkened.

Yuan had seen me like this before, laid out between two men as they pleasured me to my climax. I felt no shame then and I refused to feel it now, but deep down, my body still wanted it to be him here with me. Him above all others.

I didn't know if it was the novelty or the challenge of it that excited me. I just knew my flesh longed for his and there was no sense to it.

I will never give in to you. His declaration rung in my ears. I will never give in...

"Come here."

My throat was dry as I rasped out the command, then

held my breath. I had never issued an order I wasn't certain would be obeyed. There was no reason for Yuan to comply; he could simply turn his back and walk away and I would be left, grasping and weak. Tai and Jiyi would be there to witness my defeat. I had given Yuan power over me with that single entreaty.

"Maybe he has never been with a man before," Jiyi offered, amused. I gave him a pinch for it and he grinned, working my nipple between his fingers in return. It hardened to a peak while my skin flushed pink. Yuan watched every exchange, his expression darkening.

I was convinced he would turn on his heel in disgust, but instead he took a step toward the bed. One and then another, slow, but purposeful.

What he did next made my heart stop. I had to be dreaming.

Yuan paused by the edge of the canopy to remove his clothing, letting his tunic drop to the floor and the trousers along with it. When he climbed onto the bed, my sex flooded. Every muscle in my body weakened with desire. Jiyi could feel my response as my flesh grew lush and warm in his embrace. Tai looked at my face before leaning toward me.

He wanted to kiss me. Or rather, he wanted Yuan to see him kissing me. I wouldn't allow it. No man would make a pawn of me.

Breaking away from Jiyi and Tai, I reached for Yuan and pulled him into my arms. The other two still surrounded us as I pressed my lips against his, slipping my tongue into his mouth, my hand into his hair to hold him where I wanted him.

Yuan was hesitant at first. I could taste it in his kiss, but that soon changed. His tongue slid against mine and his breath became my breath. He started to lower me to the bed, but even while my heart pounded and my blood burned for him, I knew he didn't mean to give me what I needed. This was just another show of his resistance—he could endure whatever torment I could devise.

I turned in his arms so that my back was pressed to his chest, my head tilting up and resting against his shoulder. I could see his face from this angle and he could see mine. I could see from the torment in his eyes that I was right. Nothing had changed.

It didn't matter. I had my lovers here to satisfy my every need. I nodded toward Jiyi and he moved between my legs, parting my thighs with gentle hands.

Yuan's hands curved around my waist. I could feel their hot imprint on my skin as he spoke. "Send them away," he said roughly, almost pleading. "You don't need them."

Beside us, Tai made a derisive noise. Even Jiyi circled his thumb against the inside of my thigh, stimulating the pulse point and reminding me of all he could do for me.

"Liar," I told Yuan with a shudder. "You'll only tease me again."

Right then, Jiyi closed his hot mouth over my sex and my back arched involuntarily, my hips pushing against his tongue. He used it like a calligraphy brush, swirling the firm, wet tip of it in luscious and practiced strokes over my folds. I closed my eyes to yield to the pleasure of it.

Yuan's hands tightened on my hips. I knew he had a full view of what Jiyi was doing to me. He could feel my response as every part of me quivered and tensed. And all three could hear me, moaning.

"*Darling*," I murmured. "Yes."

Jiyi rewarded me with a series of soft, slow licks that made me want to weep. At the same time, it was Yuan who was holding me. It was the earthiness of his skin that I smelled and his cock growing to push against the cleft of my buttocks. In a wicked and perverse union, my mind combined them together into one being, created only for me.

Yuan's breathing deepened and he dragged me harder against his body. For a moment, there was a contest of wills. Yuan gripped me tight around my waist while Jiyi moved his hands onto my hips to steady me for his mouth. Ever the peacemaker, Jiyi let his hand wander upward, stroking over Yuan's forearm in invitation.

The aristocrat froze and Jiyi withdrew, though his tongue never stopped working my slit in this most intimate of kisses.

"Darling, if you don't stop, I'll come too fast," I warned, running my hands through Jiyi's thick hair as the pleasure rose higher inside me.

"Then I'll take the time to bring you back once more." His lips brushed my flesh as he spoke, making me shudder. His tongue found the soft pearl hidden in the folds and fluttered over it.

"Yes. Oh heavens, yes. *Right there*."

I opened my eyes to see Yuan staring at the other man between my legs. His chest pumped up and down rapidly. The lost look in his eyes sent me over the edge and my climax came crashing into me.

Yuan held onto me, absorbing each shudder into his own body as his hard cock throbbed against my lower back, trapped and denied.

"It feels so wonderful," I whispered to Jiyi, to Yuan. Perhaps to the heavens.

Jiyi planted a kiss against my sex while his hands kneaded my thighs lovingly. My sweet slave. But then I felt him leaving me. Tai moved to take his place between my legs. He held his erect member in one hand. It was thick with a broad head, dark with arousal and ridged with veins.

I shook my head while my hips churned restlessly. I hadn't yet come down from my first release and I knew my sex would be swollen, too tight. But Tai paid no heed to me. He knew what this would do to me. And how I liked it when he was a little cruel.

With one hand braced against my shoulder, Tai knelt between my legs. Between Yuan's legs as well as he was mirroring my pose, his legs providing a brace for mine. Tai paused with his organ pressed to my slit. I could barely breathe, waiting for the moment the thick head would breach me.

Then with one smooth thrust of his hips, he drove into me, not stopping when I cried out or when my hands reached out to push against his chest. It was reflex only.

My body wanted this invasion, even as a sob broke past my lips.

"Princess?" Yuan's voice was tight with concern. He'd removed his hands from my waist and instead settled onto my shoulders, preparing to defend me, of all things.

"It's good," I moaned brokenly. "So good."

Nothing felt like being filled by a man. And no two men were alike in this. It wasn't just the length and breadth of his cock, but so many things. His weight upon me, the sweat and salt of his skin. His smell. His taste. I'd wanted to know Yuan this way, but this half-measure was all I could have.

I dragged Yuan down to me as Tai began to pump in and out of me in small strokes.

"This is you," I told Yuan in a whisper. I could have the fantasy if I couldn't have him. "I can feel you inside me."

I kissed him, letting the taste of him take over my senses. Yuan returned the kiss hungrily and my flesh closed tight and wet around the cock that penetrated me. I imagined that it was Yuan there, driving himself into me, desiring me too much to stop himself.

Distantly, I could hear Tai groaning, the force of his thrusts increasing, but I pushed those details aside.

It was perverse and cruel to dismiss him so, but I forgot all that as my climax roared through me, harder and faster than anything I'd ever felt. I drowned in the madness of it, lost.

When I came to my senses, Yuan was no longer kissing me. His body had grown rigid, his grip tight as he fought against himself.

"Leave me, darlings," I said, keeping my eyes shut.

I had meant the command for Tai and Jiyi, but Yuan untangled his limbs from mine and retreated as well. I let him go, my body weeping silently over the loss of his warmth. I lay on my bed and listened to the pulse of my own heartbeat as it gradually quieted until there was nothing left but silence.

Late that night, I was called once again to my brother's palace.

"I saw her," he cried the moment I entered his chamber. His robe was a shambles and his hair wild about his face. One of his concubines cowered in the corner, but she appeared unharmed as far as I could see. I looked to the servants who hovered nearby for some answer, but they were all staring wide-eyed and mute.

"Who did you see?" I asked firmly. When he didn't answer, I took hold of his chin, forcing him to look at me. "Ziye, who did you see?"

"In my dreams!" he blurted out. "She was wearing white. So pale. She said I was wicked and would be dead by the next harvest."

My brother had been afraid of ghosts since he was a boy. He'd seen them in every shadow and cold breeze while I had chased them away for him. But there was no consoling him tonight. Delirious, he called for incense, for talismans. He had a sorcerer and a monk both summoned.

He was the Emperor and all we could do was indulge him.

"Light every lantern in the palace," he commanded while we waited for the first orders to be carried out.

I managed to calm him down enough for him to explain how he'd seen our deceased aunt appear before him, the one he'd beheaded because she'd refused to lie down and be violated for his amusement.

"She claimed her death was wrongful, but it was my every right," he insisted. "I am the Son of Heaven."

Yet he wore his guilt plainly on his face. He was ragged with dark circles beneath his eyes. Every noise made him jump.

"In dreams the boundary between the afterlife and our world is thin," he said desperately. "In dreams there are no guards to stop the spirits from coming for me."

By the time the shaman arrived, there was incense burning throughout the room. He chanted and waved his staff while my brother bowed before him, head to the ground. Then he spoke of how our aunt's soul had suffered an injustice and now wandered as a hungry ghost.

"You must appease her with offerings," the sorcerer counseled.

Ziye promised he would. He had an altar set up in the Bamboo Hall that night.

I had more sleeping elixir brought to my brother, this time adding a dose of opium. Ziye finally fell asleep with all the lanterns burning and Bataar stationed immediately beside his bed. The smell of camphor from the burning incense clogged the air.

With a heavy heart, I made the journey back to the East Palace. Once we left the lanterns of the main palace, there was nothing but darkness surrounding the litter. As the carriers made the last turn toward my residence, I thought of my brother and of Yuan. Only a few days ago, I had feared losing one and yearned hopelessly to possess the other.

I was only now realizing that they were both already gone.

CHAPTER NINE

When Yuan came to me midway through the next morning, I made a show of being absorbed in the letters I was writing. He stood there before the desk waiting patiently, or perhaps impatiently, I didn't know. I stared at my brush as I wrote in bold, black strokes of ink.

Had he looked over my shoulder, he would have seen the characters were nonsense. He would have seen my hand was trembling.

"Princess."

He was the first to breach the silence and I looked up to see the scroll in his hands. A heaviness settled onto my shoulders, sinking me into the floor. Let this happen quickly, I begged the heavens.

Finally, I centered my gaze onto his face. An overwhelming sense of longing swept through me. He was beautiful. As beautiful and proud as the first day I'd seen him. My heart had insisted then that he had to be mine. No other conquest was as important as this one.

It was wrong to be so obsessed with a man. This blind desire for Yuan had made me weak. He was just a man: strong shoulders, two arms, two legs. A cock hanging between them; soft or hard, depending on the circumstances.

"Why am I being banished?" he demanded, his anger barely controlled.

My stomach fluttered. I liked him angry.

Slowly, I set my brush onto the holder. "I thought you would be happy," I drawled. "I'm releasing you from my service two days early."

His jaw clenched tight. "So this is punishment."

"I tire of you. I tire of the sight of you. The thought of happening upon you in my brother's court sickens me."

My knees nearly buckled from weakness when I stood from the desk. I had to steady myself with a deep breath. In this act, I had declared myself the victor in our game. He would not be given the opportunity to refuse me and serve out his ten days. I would walk away from Yuan. I would prevail.

"The decree is clear, is it not?" I said. "You are to leave today from the capital. It was courteous of you to stop by to say farewell, but unnecessary. Be gone with you now."

With a bored expression, I retreated toward the back of the room. I could hear Yuan's strident footsteps behind me and my heart started pounding. He was upon me before I could reach the curtain.

Taking hold of me, he pressed me against a column. I could feel his chest at my back. "All of this because I wouldn't give in to your demands?"

His voice was low and dangerous in my ear. My sex flooded with wetness, but I braced my hands flat against the wood and refused to turn around. All I could think of was how he'd kissed me so hungrily the last time we were together. His erection had stabbed hard against my back as I climaxed.

When I didn't answer, I felt him tugging my skirt up. His hand stole between my legs, his fingers slipping immediately into the damp folds of my sex. My breath rushed out of me in a gasp. I closed my eyes and laid my head against the column as he rubbed roughly back and forth, drenching his fingers with my wetness.

There was no denying my body still wanted him, but I couldn't allow myself to hope he'd give in now. He'd played me long enough.

"Rescind the decree," he demanded, pressing the scroll cruelly against my cheek. Down below, he tweaked my bud between his thumb and forefinger. The effect was devastating and I couldn't hold back the sob that escaped my lips.

"It's too late," I whispered, trembling.

I would not give in. Even as pleasure radiated through me, weakening my body, my resolve remained strong.

Then Yuan did something unexpected. The hand between my legs became gentle, sliding in soothing strokes over the tortured flesh. My heart beat out of my chest as he let the scroll fall to the floor. That left both his arms free and he placed his other hand beside mine on the column. He leaned in and his body curved over mine. Warm breath fanned against my cheek.

"There is one way," he suggested in a sensual tone that sent shivers down my spine. "You can leave as well."

I stared at our hands laid side by side, struck dumb by his suggestion. "With you?" I asked breathlessly.

Below, his fingers worked delicately over my sex, stroking and slipping just inside my folds. "Leave the palace and leave Princess Shanyin behind. Then you can have me in every way."

He penetrated me with one long finger then to emphasize his point. I wanted to laugh at him that he thought his body could be worth so much, but the thrust of his finger inside me awakened an all too familiar yearning. With a sigh, I let him continue.

"What would I be, your wife?" I shouldn't have even asked that question. It gave him too much power.

Yuan's hand stilled between my legs. "That isn't possible."

I swung around and his fingers slid out of me. "You would have me give away my royal position, and not even for the meager protection of your name?"

Yuan remained close and unwavering, trapping me against the column in a near embrace.

"The very thing that you believe protects you, endangers you," he warned.

"I see. You have to cast yourself in the role of my savior in order to fuck me. How tiresome."

My sharp words failed to wound him. Instead his face softened as he regarded me. "I didn't want to care for you."

The ache in my heart was too much for me to bear. How much did he know of my brother's atrocities? Of how volatile the Emperor had become?

"I know being princess puts me in danger," I replied quietly. "I've been in danger all my life."

"But you can escape. You gave Sparrow a choice. Now you can make that choice for yourself."

"Little Sparrow?" I was surprised he even remembered my brother's pitiful concubine.

I had sent the girl to a monastery so she could escape my brother's cruelty, but there was no such escape for me. What did Yuan expect me to do, leave the palace and shave my head? Live the rest of my life in self-denial? I was stupid to have wavered, even for a second.

"I am Princess Shanyin and always will be." I tilted my chin up to meet his eyes squarely. "And you have been ordered to leave the capital."

He held my gaze for a long time, leaning close. For a moment, I thought he would kiss me, but he straightened.

"Farewell, Princess," he said softly.

My chest hitched. I was only imagining the tender look in his eyes.

"This is the last I will ever see of you," I told him without a hint of emotion.

That was how I ended our nine-day dance of seduction. With Yuan walking away while I watched him go.

My spies reported to me immediately after Yuan left the capital city that same day. He was accompanied by an entourage of servants with all his belongings packed into trunks. I'd found another appointment for him near the coast. I imagined it would be beautiful there with the ocean spread out before him. Maybe he would even think of me during the long journey.

As soon as I was certain Yuan was gone, a sense of emptiness overwhelmed me. I took out the bamboo brush that I'd kept hidden in my sleeve and ran it gently over the inside of my wrist, feeling tears gather at the corners of my eyes.

It was the fine-haired brush Yuan had tormented me with that day at the hot springs. I'd saved it, secretly hiding it in my robe. I imagined his bold hand wielding the instrument now. Teasing me until I wept with frustrated pleasure.

My thoughts were interrupted by a visitor. It was my brother's personal bodyguard, Bataar. He bowed when brought before me and regarded me gravely with his one good eye.

"You told me to inform you, Princess, if there was any more trouble."

At his words, my heart sank. I followed Bataar out to the wagon he'd driven from the palace. There was a single trunk in the back. The kind used to store clothes. Even though he didn't want to obey, I commanded the bodyguard to open it.

A woman's body had been shoved inside, curled up tight. I imagined she was one of my brother's servants or concubines.

"Close it," I said quickly. Bile rose in my throat.

Bataar did as I asked and helped me down from the

wagon. "The Emperor strangled her because she resembled the other woman he had put to death," he explained. "Then he told me to get rid of the body."

It would have been pointless to protest that the woman hadn't resembled our aunt in the least. Maybe we were all starting to look alike to my brother.

"Bury her properly," I told Bataar. He bowed again and left to do my bidding.

That night my brother asked me to stay in the imperial quarters with him. He was pale and shaken. I took one of the rooms adjacent to his bedchamber and was woken up in the middle night by his screams.

"She's back! I see her. *I see her.*"

I bypassed the sleeping elixir and gave him opium tea directly. He required two doses before he would calm down enough to sleep. Afterward I lay awake in my bed, shivering even though the night was warm.

Did Yuan truly think I didn't know how dangerous my brother was? With one wild impulse, Ziye could have me beheaded and then weep over my lifeless body afterward. But if I abandoned him, no one would remain to control his murderous whims.

The high-ranking eunuchs didn't care. As long as a weak Emperor sat on the throne, they could do as they pleased. The powerful ministers of the court all feared being the first to be made an example of. Why risk their positions for the lives of a few pitiful concubines and palace women?

Yuan would never know the real reason I'd sent him

from the palace. My brother was becoming angry, jealous and violent. Of all my lovers, there was only one he knew by name. And Ziye had already accused me of wanting to run away with Yuan.

If I had gone with him today, the Emperor would have found us. He would cut off Yuan's organ and feed it to wild dogs while Yuan bled to death.

Let Yuan believe I'd exiled him as punishment for refusing me. Men were nearsighted by nature, cursed to only see one side of every story.

CHAPTER TEN

The next morning, Ziye gathered three hundred of his palace women all dressed in white to congregate in the Bamboo Hall. I walked beside him as the procession traveled through the imperial park. The atmosphere was solemn. Not a single word was spoken the entire way.

The white robe I wore reminded me of a mourning garment. The last time I'd dressed in white was for my father's funeral. Ziye had been crowned Emperor shortly after. Had it only been a year ago?

Four shamans were waiting for us inside the building. Ziye had decided one was not enough; he required four. They each wore ritual headdresses and strange clothing with almost a tribal appearance. Together, they chanted a wailing tune that hurt my ears.

Ziye fell to his knees before them and the rest of the procession did the same. The vast hall fit all three hundred of us with room to spare. My brother had ordered his guards to stand back and remain outside. He feared the swords would anger the ghosts—as if his very presence wouldn't upset them.

I bit my tongue and kept all my thoughts to myself. I hoped these shamans were skilled enough to make Ziye believe.

"There are ghosts in this hall!" one shaman proclaimed in a singsong voice. The others echoed his cry. *Ghosts in this hall.*

"We will banish them today so they will no longer haunt the earth."

There was the clang of cymbals and the beat of drums. The head shaman presented a bow and four arrows to my brother. He was to shoot the ghosts, one in each corner of the hall, and then music would be played to clear out the spirits.

Ziye stood and I could see his hands were shaking as he took the bow. His face was pale and drawn and there were deep circles beneath his eyes. With one look at me, he moved to the center of the room. The shaman pointed to one corner of the room while he chanted away and my brother pulled back the bow and fired the first arrow. Then the shaman repeated the process in the next corner and the next.

With each arrow, my brother seemed to strengthen. He no longer trembled as he aimed the last arrow into the corner. It occurred to me then that Ziye needed to be afraid of something to keep him contained. Maybe this ghost-catching ritual wasn't a good thing.

As the last arrow flew, one of the woman broke away from the sea of white and ran toward Ziye. That was when I realized it wasn't a woman, but a man. One of Ziye's closest retainers. He dragged a dagger out of his robe.

The bodyguards were all outside.

Ziye tried to run. The palace women all scattered, but I was still kneeling on the floor. My limbs wouldn't move.

I watched as the assailant caught up with my brother and thrust the dagger into his chest. The hand holding the blade withdrew and thrust again. My brother slumped over, the front of his white robe stained with blood. The palace women swarmed all around me like a flight of cranes.

White on white on white, then red.

I rose to my feet, my head spinning. My brother's gaze roamed through the crowd until he found me. His eyes were impossibly wide as he stretched out his hand. That was his final expression and his last act. Looking at me, pleading with me for something as he died. Whatever it was, I would never know.

Did we not always say our fates were linked, you and I?

Armed men finally entered the hall, but I realized they weren't my brother's bodyguards. It was Bataar who grabbed me. The sight of his ragged face brought me back to my senses; he was easily recognizable.

"Rebels," he told me. "It's an uprising."

Throughout the hall there was shouting, running, confusion, blood. The imperial guards had stormed inside as well as rebel fighters. I didn't know who was on what side. It looked as if everyone was striking out at everyone else. Women in white lay crumpled to the floor.

There were ghosts in this hall. More ghosts by the moment.

"The Emperor is dead," I told Bataar listlessly, my voice floating in from far away.

He stared at me with his one eye. The clouded one seemed to look past me.

"You must come with me now, Princess." He drew his broadsword and took me by the arm. "This will only get worse."

A rebel faction was gathered outside of the Bamboo Hall, but Bataar and the other bodyguards fought through them. Blood splattered over his uniform and onto me as well as he swung his sword with one arm and dragged me forward with the other.

When we were free of the imperial park I saw fighting had broken out in the palace. I heard the name Liu Yu spoken over and over. One of the uncles in cages, who I had insisted Ziye free.

"Take me to the East Palace," I told Bataar.

"Princess—"

"Do it," I commanded gently.

Bataar cleared the way for me to return to my residence while the other bodyguards joined up with the palace guards. Their loyalty was to the Emperor, not to me.

I had survived more than one palace coup and I knew what came in the aftermath. Perhaps this was why I found myself so eerily calm while the world burned around me. I could tell that news had reached the East Palace because the servants were frantic when I arrived. Everyone started asking me questions all at once: "What do we do? What do we do?"

"Leave now. Run away," I said, partly because it was likely their only chance of escaping, but also because I couldn't stand their wailing any longer.

I opened all my coffers and spilled my jewels onto the floor of my quarters. "Take it all. Bribe anyone you can to get free."

The maidservants wept. Some of them didn't want to leave and huddled in their rooms. Others filled their skirts with jewels and fled.

"You should escape now as well, Princess." Bataar's rough voice startled me as I stood alone in my dressing room. "While the imperial guard are still fighting."

I smiled sadly at him and shook my head. "There will be no escape for me."

Retainers had already assassinated the cruel and vindictive Emperor. His depraved and immoral sister was soon to follow. This was how old regimes were toppled and new ones propped up. I had seen this happen again and again.

"Do not lose heart, Princess. We may be able to regain control."

Who would have thought that this fearsome beast of a man would harbor such an optimistic soul? Again I shook my head. "It won't happen."

No one would stand up to rally the imperial forces in the wake of my brother's death. Ziye had left no sons behind and his closest adviser had been myself, a more unsuitable ruler than he was. This was the end of our line.

"Then if the princess would accept my service. I would

swear my loyalty to her until my very last breath."

The warrior sank to one knee, head lowered. He had been my brother's servant, not mine, yet here he was pledging undying loyalty to me in my final hour. I couldn't help but be touched.

"Allow this servant the privilege of dying in your defense," Bataar requested. I hesitated before reaching out to touch his shoulder.

"That privilege should be ours."

It was Tai who spoke. He came into the parlor with a trail of men behind him. A fist closed painfully around my heart when I saw that they were all assembled together; all thirty of my beautiful lovers.

"Please go, all of you," I implored. "Escape now while you can. I don't want to have your deaths on my soul."

I turned away, unable to look at them. So much beauty wasted. My eyes stung and I couldn't bear for them to see my tears.

At first, no one would leave me. But as news of the rebellion became worse, they began to depart in twos and threes. I wished them all peace and hoped that at least a few of them would survive. I really did care for them—it was hard not to when they had been dedicated to the singular task of pleasing me.

Tai and Jiyi were the last to remain. Bataar had departed with the last set. He was a warrior who deserved to die fighting.

"Go," I commanded my two favorites gently. "Promise me you'll survive and find a pair of pretty and innocent girls to seduce into a blissful marriage."

"But Princess, how can we leave you?" Jiyi's eyes were filled with tears.

"We will stay with you until the end," Tai insisted.

I went to them, kissing each of them tenderly on the lips. "You've given me such great joy. Please leave me to make my own peace with my ancestors. This is my final wish."

It might seem like I was being kind and selfless, but that wasn't true. I couldn't bear having to witness their deaths while I was preparing to meet mine.

They finally turned to go, walking side by side, and I was left alone in the eerie silence of my palace where I had indulged in every earthly pleasure I knew. The only decision that remained was where I would be found when the rebellion came for me.

I considered lying down on my legendary bed, but I didn't wish to sully the good memories I had of it now that my harem was gone. Instead, I went to my flower garden to sit among the blooms and let their perfume surround me.

There are only a few ways a woman can be remembered. History might have immortalized me as a pawn, or a victim. A poor unfortunate princess who was brutalized by the whims of more powerful men. I chose instead to be remembered as a woman of pleasure whose lust knew no bounds. These scars on my back, the nameless men who took me to their beds—it was all by my design, for my own enjoyment. That was how I chose to remember it. This was how I mastered my nightmares.

I would not be haunted by the past. There were no such things as ghosts.

In the end it wasn't men with swords who came for me. Only one lone figure entered the garden and as soon as I saw him, I had all the answers I had been missing.

Yuan came to stand before me while I sat surrounded by clusters of jasmine. My heart beat harder in his presence. My skin flushed and came alive. I must have been deranged after all to still respond this way even when I knew the truth.

"You were part of the rebellion all along, weren't you?" I asked him.

"Yes."

"Is it over yet?"

"It is."

He didn't appear triumphant as he regarded me. As always, his look was one of turmoil.

"My dear Yuan, you should have simply taken me to bed," I chided. "You could have fucked any secret you wanted out of me."

"No, Princess. I couldn't."

The sincerity in his voice tore me in two. The reason for his stalwart refusal had also become clear. Yuan didn't want to make unspoken promises with his body that he would later have to break.

"How wonderfully honorable of you. Let me guess, is Chancellor Wu also part of the rebellion? That was why you were so mortified when he saw me using you to satisfy my lust. And Liu Shang as well as the other uncles, of course."

Yuan remained impervious to my taunting, but there was no need for him to get angry. He'd won.

"They know that you intervened to spare their lives," he said.

"And I'm sure they will now reward me handsomely for it," I replied with a snort.

He came closer until he stood immediately before me, his shadow blocking the setting sun. "You have been accused of immorality and sentenced to commit suicide."

I hated how he spoke without emotion. I hated even more that he brought tears to my eyes. I would have rather had my death proclaimed by someone I cared nothing for.

His speech became less formal, his tone softer. "Allowing you to take your own life seemed preferable to...the other options."

I laughed, feeling madness setting in. "So this is their kindness. And you're here to ensure the deed is done?"

Finally Yuan appeared regretful, perhaps even sad. "Yes, Princess."

It wasn't as if I could escape. The entire palace had been taken over. Within the day, the imperial court would be swearing loyalty to a new Emperor.

"Is there any final preparation you require?" he asked quietly.

I looked down at my clothes. For the first time, I realized I was still wearing the white robe from the ghost-catching ceremony, but it had been splattered with blood.

"I would like to change clothes."

He nodded solemnly. Together we left the garden to return to my quarters. All of my attendants had fled or were in hiding, so I went to my wardrobe myself. I ended up selecting the same silk robe I'd worn on our trip to the hot springs and wondered if Yuan even remembered. The gold shawl was still missing. Was it still in his possession? Did he inhale my scent while he brought himself to climax?

"All my maidservants are gone," I told him.

Without a word, Yuan moved to help me undress and put on the clean robe. His touch was impersonal, refusing to linger. His eyes avoided mine.

Even now, he denied me and left me wanting, though I was no longer seeking sexual release. All I wanted was a kind look or a soft touch. I knew I was undeserving, but I was still greedy.

When we returned to the sitting room, a messenger stood there with a tray in hand. A single cup of tea sat on the tray. I didn't have to ask what was in it.

Yuan gestured for the poison to be left upon the table. The messenger disappeared promptly and we were alone once more. There was no need to draw out the inevitable any longer.

"Will you stay until I'm sleeping?" I asked him. When in our brief time together had I ever requested anything of him?

At first Yuan didn't answer. He looked at me the same way he had when he'd said farewell—was that only a day ago? His look was soft, almost tender. "I will, Princess," he said finally, his voice rough with emotion.

"Once I'm gone, will you make sure no one is allowed to cut up my body? Or...or my face?" My voice was so small it was barely there.

"I won't let anyone touch you," he vowed. Then he added, very gently. "I never knew you to be so vain."

I tried to smile. "You called me beautiful once."

All of a sudden, his arms were around me, warm and secure. His mouth found mine and for the first time he kissed me passionately, without reservation. My knees weakened and I sagged against him, returning his kiss with my entire being.

He didn't take me to my bed; to the place where so many other men had served and pleasured me. Instead he lowered me right there onto the floor while I tore at his clothes. Before long, there was a pile of silk surrounding us and his hand was cupped between my legs. I bit into my lower lip to keep from moaning as he eased a finger inside me.

I had to be perverse to already be so aroused, even now at the brink of death. Especially now, but I was. Every nerve in my body was crying out for one more climax, one more perfect moment. And I had waited so long for Yuan, wondering how he would feel when we were joined together.

Reaching up, I wrapped my hand around his cock and watched his face as I stroked him from base to tip.

"I thought about you every night," he groaned. "Every night I spilled desperately into my hand, dreaming of you." He closed his eyes as I worked his shaft. "You weaken me," he muttered. "You weaken me, you weaken me."

We didn't bother with any preliminaries. The last nine days had been foreplay and our patience was spent. Yuan shoved my hand aside and entered me in one long, endless penetration that left me breathless. I closed my eyes to shut out everything but him. He thrust again and my body squeezed tight around him to hold on to the sensation. I knew it would be this good. Oh heaven, I knew.

In three hard thrusts, he had me coming with stars in my eyes. My back arched so forcefully that I thought I would snap in two.

My only regret was that it had happened so fast when I wanted so much for it to last. As I came back to my senses, I realized Yuan was still hard inside me. He withdrew and I moaned as he pulled out, my body sensitive in the aftermath.

Before I could catch my breath, he flipped me over. With my hands braced against the floor, he lifted my hips and entered me from behind, his cock piercing me from a different angle. I cried out, overwhelmed with what he was doing to me. Each thrust brought me to a new height and soon I was close again.

How could this be? How could I reach orgasm so readily when I knew it would be my last?

I didn't have time for such worthless questions. All I had time for was this. Pleasure had always been my escape. I swam in it now. My time was measured and this was the last memory I wanted to take with me to the afterlife. Not regret or sadness or anguish over the cruelty of fate. I wanted to remember the warmth of Yuan's skin and the indescribable feeling of him deep inside me, fucking, fucking, fucking me into oblivion.

When he first entered me from this position I thought he was avoiding having to look me in the eye, knowing what would have to happen afterward. But that wasn't it. He shortened his movements until they became a second heartbeat, pulsing in and out of me. Then he lowered himself and I could feel his lips pressing against the scars on my back, one after another.

"Please come now," I urged. "Come inside me."

A moment later, he did, spilling his essence deep against my womb as I joined him in a climax that started in my sex but radiated out until my whole body shook and spasmed.

Afterward, the sound of our breathing combined in an uneven cadence and his weight grew heavy over me as we both sagged into the floor. I thought it was done until his hand closed over mine.

"It has to be this way," he said regretfully.

I closed my eyes. "I know."

He wasn't betraying my trust. I had known what would happen, but I wanted him anyway.

Yuan rolled over on his back and I crawled over to curl myself against his side and lay my head on his chest. For a few precious moments, I listened to the sound of his heartbeat.

There was no better time than now, while my body was sated and warm from our lovemaking. I could wait and cling onto every last breath, but for what purpose? That would only give time for regret to sink in.

I rose from the floor and stood, looking down at Yuan. He propped himself up on one arm to watch me. I appreciated how he was put together in clean lines and hard shapes. For the last ten days, I had obsessed about possessing him and now I had, in the most bittersweet of ways. Perhaps I had known Ziye's tyranny would have to come to an end. I wanted to seek my own selfish pleasure until my last breath.

With that one final look enclosed in my heart, I went to the table and picked up the cup. By now, the tea was cold. I lifted it and took the poison into myself the same way I'd approached life: swallowing it whole without looking back.

There was sweetness on top of the bitterness. Someone had laced the brew with honey, a small kindness. It made me smile.

I returned to Yuan's arms then and he accepted me, holding me tight and stroking my hair. Sleep came quickly after that and I didn't try to fight it.

"I'm glad you're here with me," I told him, my words starting to slur together.

"I insisted. I wouldn't leave you to anyone else."

Closing my eyes, I snuggled into him. I willed myself to believe that I really was only falling asleep so I could go without fear. Yuan would be waiting there for me when I woke up and, because there would be no one to tell me otherwise, I convinced myself that he really did love me, just a little bit.

EPILOGUE

In the afterlife, I saw my brother. Ziye was wandering around in an endless gray. I could hear the mumble of voices all around us but I saw no one else. He was still wearing the white robe with a bloodstain at his chest where the dagger had struck. His face was pale and gaunt.

"I'm hungry," he told me.

I looked around, but there was no food. There was nothing. Our family had fostered a tradition of killing one another and there was no one left to light incense or honor us with offerings of rice and fruit. Such was the fate of those poor souls who died without any offspring. Who had been disowned by our families. We were left to wander forever as hungry ghosts.

"I'm hungry," he repeated, his voice sounding hollow and lost. "I'm hungry."

There was nothing I could do for my brother. Desperately, I reached into my chest and pulled out my own heart, still beating faintly, and fed it to him.

Light came in flashes, hurting my eyes. I squinted against it, finally forcing my lids open enough to see something besides gray.

I was wrapped in a large blanket or bolt of cloth. There was a cover over my head and I pulled it away, catching a glimpse of trees overhead and a wagon around me before the cover was yanked back in place.

"Princess, we're still in danger. You can't be seen," a voice whispered.

I thought I knew that voice, but I couldn't identify it through the fog in my head.

As the wagon rolled on, I began to piece things together. I was still alive. There were two men in the wagon with me, one in the driver's seat and another beside me. I wasn't bound, but I could barely move. My limbs were stiff and my stomach rolled as if I were going to be sick.

"It's Jiyi," the voice beside me whispered and my heart nearly burst with joy.

A long time later, the wagon stopped and Jiyi unwound me from the bundle of silk I'd been hidden inside. I had figured out who his companion must be. Tai unhitched the horses and tethered them while Jiyi tended to the fire.

"I told you to leave me," I scolded them as I climbed down from the wagon.

Tai flashed me a crooked smile, cutting through the weariness on his face. "The princess likes me best when I disobey."

I had so many questions to ask them, but all the emotions I'd been holding back flooded into me all at once. I bent over, sobbing with my arms wrapped around myself. I was alive and Yuan...Yuan hadn't sent me to my death after all. The tea had contained a strong sedative rather than poison. Yet he'd played a cruel trick on me by not telling me.

Despite only having spent ten days with Yuan, I understood him so well now. He wanted me to suffer at least the fear of death. There were consequences to my pleasure-seeking, to my selfish neglect of right and wrong. I knew then that he truly did hate me. But that he loved me as well.

"Princess?" Jiyi addressed me tentatively.

I raised my head to see the two of them looking at me, uncertain what to do. They'd never seen me crying before.

"I'm no longer your princess," I corrected, wiping my eyes.

Princess Shanyin was dead. The only life I'd known was gone and I had no sense of who I was or what my life would be like from here. With a deep breath, I took a step toward my two former concubines to discover what this new existence would be.

The story of Princess Shanyin continues in *The Enslavement*, available online. *Princess Shanyin: The Complete Obsession Series (Book 1-3)* is also available in print or digital.

ACKNOWLEDGMENTS

Thank you to my awesome production team: Jodi Henley, Julia Ganis, and Dana Waganer for embarking on this adventure with me. And special thanks to Shawntelle Madison for all the extra hand holding.

ABOUT THE AUTHOR

LILIANA LEE writes erotic stories set in exotic worlds. The Princess Shanyin series is her erotic debut.

Liliana also writes romantic and speculative fiction as Jeannie Lin.

She can be found online at http://www.lilianalee.com. Go to website for more information and to sign up for updates.